Troy

Troy

An American Extreme Bull Riders Tour Romance

Amy Andrews

Troy

Copyright © 2017 Amy Andrews
Tule Publishing First Printing, August 2017
The Tule Publishing Group, LLC

ALL RIGHTS RESERVED

No part of this book may be used or reproduced in any manner whatsoever without written permission except in the case of brief quotations embodied in critical articles and reviews.

This is a work of fiction. Names, characters, places, and incidents are products of the author's imagination or are used fictitiously. Any resemblance to actual events, locales, organizations, or persons, living or dead, is entirely coincidental.

ISBN: 978-1-947636-37-8

Chapter One

Joss Garrity was not having a very good day. In fact she'd not been having a very good five years. Dead husband, teenage son who hated her, astronomical student loan debt and almost as astronomical orthodontic bills. Not to mention a sleep deficit she'd never make up even if she slept from now until the end of the decade.

And, this just in, a flat tire. With the stubbornest set of wheel nuts she'd ever had the misfortune to tangle with.

She turned her eyes toward the star-littered sky. "Just once," she begged, "give me a break."

She crouched beside the wheel again and fitted the lug wrench to the nut via the weak beam of a flashlight. Putting her full weight behind it she pushed. *Hard.*

It didn't move. Not even a fraction.

A well of frustration geysered out of her and she sprung up yelling, "*Aaaaaah!*" striking the stubborn nut over and over with the wrench.

It didn't help but it felt damn good. The clanking noise echoed around the surrounding cornfields and she didn't stop until the sudden slice of oncoming headlights alerted her to an approaching car. Breathing heavily, she threw the wrench on the ground.

Apart from the sound of a decelerating engine, the night had fallen quiet around her as if even the insects had been startled into silence by her outburst. She supposed they didn't get too many crazy women attacking car tires at almost midnight—or anytime really—in these parts.

The car, some kind of pickup, pulled up behind her. The engine cut out; the lights didn't. She squinted against their intrusion as the car door opened, then shut. A figure approached, tall and shadowy, his cowboy hat haloed by light.

A man.

With a lazy gait. The soft crunch of his boots on the dirt road, unhurried. One shoulder hitched slightly higher than the other. She supposed she should be afraid it was some psycho serial killer haunting the back roads of Texas. The way her luck had been running it'd be par for the course.

But nothing that dramatic ever happened around here. It'd just be one of the locals doing the neighborly thing. Even if most folks in these parts would usually have been bedded down this late on a Wednesday night.

"That's an interesting technique for changing a tire."

The voice, as lazy and unhurried as his stride, came out at her from the night a second before the shadows revealed the man in all his glory.

Tall. Rangy. Jeans. Big-ass buckle. Checked flannel shirt, the sleeves rolled up to the elbows. She couldn't see his face—between the brim of his hat and the back lighting it was still firmly in shadow—but she knew he wasn't a local.

Not with that accent.

It was as lazy and unhurried as the rest of him, his vowels flattened. Joss could detect a slight American twang but he definitely hadn't been born here.

English. Or New Zealand. Maybe Australian.

He came to a halt, slipping his hands into his back pockets, the stance widening his chest.

"How about you let me do that?"

Joss waited for the *little lady* but it wasn't forthcoming. *Hallelujah*. She'd had enough of men today and right now she didn't need any he-man bull crap. The fact that she needed him at all totally blew.

"I'm perfectly able to change my own goddamn tire." She glared in the general direction of his shadowed face.

It wasn't the first tire she'd changed and she doubted it'd be her last. Not to mention she was a freaking ER doctor. She could drill a burr hole in his head, crack open his chest, stitch him up again and bring him back to life with a spot of CPR all on the side of this road if she had to.

Not that thinking about putting her mouth over his was particularly helpful right now.

"Well okay then." He lifted a shoulder. "Don't let me stop you."

Joss sighed. "I can't. Not this time." At five feet four she had to tilt her head to look at him and that pissed her off too. "I can't get the wheel nuts off. They're being recalcitrant like all the men hereabouts."

He laughed. And damn if it wasn't lazy too. Rich and heavy, oozing over her like warm honey. How could something so laid-back have such a quickening effect on her pulse?

"Lug nuts are dudes?"

"These ones are."

"I'm guessing belting the shit of them didn't help."

"Well that depends on your definition of help. It made me feel a hell of a lot better."

That laugh again. Sliding slow and easy from his lips. Goose bumps pricked at her arms and her nipples tightened in her bra despite the warmth of the July night. For a crazy moment she imagined him stepping in closer and brushing a soft kiss against the shallow dip at the base of her throat.

Great. Now she was fantasizing—*sexually*—about a complete stranger who'd stopped to help her with her tire.

Get a grip, Joss.

"I get that."

Joss had the distinct impression this man *got* a lot of things. "Why in hell do they screw them on so tight?" she demanded.

She was no weakling. People came to her when they wanted difficult jars opened, for Pete's sake.

"They use a pneumatic tightener."

"Because giving people roadside hernias is funny to

them?"

The brief flash of white teeth told her she'd amused him. He removed his hands from his pockets. "Would you like me to have a go?"

Joss sighed in defeat. It was that or call the Triple A service and God knew how long it'd take to get someone out here. It'd be after one—if she was lucky—by the time she got home and sleep was a precious enough commodity as it was. At least, with the summer vacation here she didn't have to worry about the daily tug-of-war involved in getting Damien out of bed.

"If you could just loosen the nuts, I can handle the rest."

Without another word he stepped around her, crouching beside the wheel as she had done, picking up the wrench. His headlights beamed across the tips of his dusty cowboy boots, along the lean length of his thigh and illuminated his face.

Joss sucked in a breath. *Sweet baby cheeses.* He was a baby. Younger than she'd thought. *Way* younger than that very adult laugh had suggested.

His jaw was strong and cleanly shaven. Ridiculously long eyelashes cast shadows over well-defined cheekbones. His mouth, despite being fixed in a line of concentration, hinted at fullness *and* experience. A tiny white scar bisected his left eyebrow, giving him a rather rakish appearance, and a crooked nose dirtied up the symmetry of his face.

He was maybe...mid twenties.

Mid *twenties.*

And she'd... Her cheeks warmed at her earlier thoughts and the persistent tautness of her nipples.

It took less than thirty seconds and a few X-rated grunts from him to loosen the nuts. *Of course.*

"Thank you," Joss said, taking a step toward him. "I can take it from here." She just wanted him gone now. Before her nipples embarrassed her any further. She felt inadequate enough lately without adding dirty old woman to her list of faults.

He slid the jack beneath the frame. "I'm down here now," he dismissed, as he cranked the handle and the car started to rise off the ground. "Might as well go all the way."

Joss shut her eyes as his words conjured other things he could do while he was *down there*. Oh God. She was going to hell. "It's fine, *really*," she insisted.

But he ignored her as he set about fixing the flat. A tanned forearm caught the light, contracting under the weight of the tire, and she stared at its perfection. Not big, gym-junkie meaty, just nicely delineated, finely honed.

God...why had men with nice arms always been her weakness? Why couldn't she be an abs or ass woman?

"So what are you doing out here?" she asked, as he grabbed the spare she'd already dragged out of the trunk.

She had to say something to keep a whole lot of unwanted thoughts at bay and he clearly wasn't from around here. This was no highway. It was a tiny back road usually only traversed by locals who knew where they were going.

Maybe he was lost?

"What am *I* doing out here?"

His thorough gaze trekked from her shoes all the way up to meet her eyes. Joss's breath practically stopped in her chest at the full impact of his illuminated face.

"What the hell is a lone woman doing out here at midnight?"

"I'm a doctor. I was…seeing a patient."

"At midnight?"

Joss sighed. "It's a long story."

Involving another stubborn man. One of Gus's friends whose wife had rung at ten begging Joss to come out and stitch up her husband who'd cut his hand and was refusing to go to hospital.

If it had been up to her she'd have let the old coot alone but his wife's distress over imminent exsanguination had played on Joss's conscience. Andy, her dead husband, had laughingly called it her doctor bone.

She'd always been crap at ignoring it.

"And you?" she pressed.

He returned his attention to the wheel. "I'm just—" He grunted slightly as he lifted the new tire onto the rim, the tip of his tongue poking out as he threaded it through the nuts. "Passing through."

Passing through where? Back-road USA? Was he a tourist? "You're not from around here, are you?"

He gave a half laugh. "No, ma'am."

Even the way he'd ma'am'ed her sounded foreign on his tongue. "You're English."

"No bloody way." He gave a derisive snort as he loosely screwed the wheel nuts in place.

"New Zealander."

"Kiwi." Another snort. "Closer. *Better*."

Joss smiled. "Australian."

"Born and bred."

Australia. She'd always wanted to visit Australia. "You're a long way from home."

He shrugged. "Home's wherever I lay my hat."

So he was a wanderer. A rolling stone…

He made quick work of lowering the car to the ground before reaching for the lug wrench again and tightening the nuts properly. He grunted with the exertion, which did bad, bad things to her overactive imagination.

And even worse things to her overheated body.

"Don't do them too tight or I'll have the same problem next time."

He laughed again, low and lazy, and it brushed up her body. "While I'm flattered you think I have the strength of a pneumatic power tool, I don't. And the last thing you need is to have your wheel fall off while you're driving along." He patted the tire. "There. Good as new."

Before she could thank him, he'd risen from the ground in one languid movement with her flat, the jack and the lug wrench and was heading toward the trunk. She followed him although she had no idea why.

His headlights flooded him from behind, once again throwing his face into shadow but she could easily see the white slash of his eyebrow scar. For a moment she wondered how he got it. For an even crazier moment she wanted to reach out and smooth it with her finger.

Thankfully he was oblivious to her insane impulses, as he slotted the wheel into the spare tire compartment and stowed the jack and the lug wrench. "Make sure you get this fixed first thing."

"Of course," she said as he shut the trunk, irritated by his need to state the obvious and the crazy urge to touch him pulsing through her hands.

"Are you from round here?" He rested his hip against the trunk as he wiped his hands on the ass of his jeans. He didn't seem to be in any kind of hurry to leave and suddenly, despite the hour, Joss wasn't either.

"Plainview. About fifty miles away."

He nodded. "That's where I'm heading."

So he wasn't just passing through. "Staying for a while?"

"Five nights. I'm riding bulls at the rodeo on the weekend."

The rodeo was this weekend? Damn it, she'd forgotten. *Awesome.* Joss guessed patching up a parade of cowboys was in her future.

"That's kinda dangerous."

He laughed as if being trampled to death or sustaining a

serious injury via a one-ton bull was of no particular consequence. "That's not the standard female reaction."

She blinked at his teasing tone and she wondered if this guy ever took anything seriously. "Oh? You were after breathless admiration?"

His teeth flashed again. "Something like that."

"Yeah, I'm not really good at breathless admiration."

"No shit." His laugh hooted out into the night, echoing around the fields.

"I'm guessing that's how you got this, right?"

Ignoring the obvious deviation of what once must have been a very nice nose, Joss finally gave in to the impulse to touch his eyebrow. The pad of her finger tingled as it brushed against bristly hair and smooth scar tissue.

She'd done it without thinking about the appropriateness of it but…she was a doctor. It was just a…*doctor* thing.

Doctors touched, prodded, examined.

But he wasn't a patient and it didn't feel very medical. It felt very, *very* sexual. The dark of the night, the hush of the fields loaned an intimacy to the situation that was as tangible as it was surprising.

"Maybe." His gaze was hooded but fixed on hers, his voice gravelly.

Joss drew in a shaky breath and dropped her hand. How had they come to be standing so close? She took a step back.

"Well…anyway…thank you for stopping to help but I really should be going now."

He didn't move or protest, just watched her, his gaze riveting. She couldn't really see his eyes but she could *feel* them on her.

"You should come and watch me."

She frowned. "Watch you?"

A small smiled nudged his lips. She didn't need to be a mind reader to know where his mind had just gone. "Ride bulls. On the weekend."

There were probably about a hundred things she'd put her hand up to watch this guy do, a lot of them just as dirty as the things he'd been thinking. Watching him get tossed around for entertainment on the back of a large angry animal wasn't one of them. "I can't. I'm working from two to eleven."

"That's a shame. Maybe we could…" He hit her with a slow, lazy smile. "Catch up for a drink after you finish work."

It might have been a long time since Joss had dated but a guy asking you out for a late-night drink wasn't usually interested in *catching up*. In fact if that wasn't code for booty call she didn't know what was.

She had no doubt there'd be a hundred girls his age who'd meet him any damn time he wanted but she was a single mother of a teenage son and she was juggling too many balls.

She didn't have time for booty calls.

"A drink?" She hoped he could read the sardonic intent

of her cocked eyebrow in the dark.

His grin told her he did. "Sure. Or—" He shrugged. "Whatever."

Joss didn't think *whatever* meant going to see a movie. She supposed she should be insulted to be propositioned at the side of the road by someone she barely knew. Or at least a little apprehensive about her vulnerability out here alone. But she was neither. If anything it was doing her downtrodden ego the world of good.

But…she was a practical woman.

She folded her arms. "Are you flirting with me?"

"That depends." He pushed the brim of his hat back a little with his index finger. "Is it working?"

Joss laughed. Actually *laughed*. Was it working? Hell to the yeah. Nevertheless, the fact that this boy-man found *her* attractive was ludicrous. She was already failing at adulting without adding *whatever* into her to-do list.

"How old are you?"

"Twenty-seven."

Twenty-seven. *Older than she'd thought.* But still… "I'm thirty-four."

He lifted a shoulder. "So?"

So? Joss sighed. "That's seven years older than you."

He grinned. "Seven years more experienced."

Joss suppressed the urge to laugh hysterically. If he thought he'd be getting some kind of well-honed tantric experience from her, he'd be sorely let down. She was too damn tired to be some kind of Mrs. Robinson.

Like he even needed one.

"Look, you're very sweet—"

His dramatic wince interrupted her. "Is there where you pat me on the head and tell me to run along now?"

It was Joss's turn to laugh. "Something like that."

"Are you sure I can't interest you?" He set his broad grin to stun. "I'm really *very* good with my hands."

Joss didn't doubt it. "To which my flat tire can attest. But trust me, there are plenty of pretty girls your age in town who would happily volunteer for a demonstration."

And Joss was blindingly envious of every one of them.

He slid his hands into his back pockets and set his jaw. "What if I don't want a girl? What if I want a woman?"

Chapter Two

JOSS'S BREATH HITCHED at the sudden seriousness to his tone. He suddenly didn't seem twenty-seven. He seemed old beyond his years. Her arms prickled with goose bumps and her nipples scrunched into tight points.

God. He was *so* damn enticing. She'd never been tempted to drag a stranger into her car and do him on the side of the road at midnight.

Never.

But she was now. Except she didn't do crap like that.

"Well…" Joss clawed her way back from the edge. "There are plenty of them as well."

He looked like he was going to push some more but then he shrugged and smiled. The guy obviously knew to quit while he was ahead. After all, there were plenty more fish in the sea for someone young and cocky and bulletproof.

"Can't blame a guy for trying, right?"

Joss shook her head at his unabashed statement. "I guess not."

"Troy." He held out his hand. "Troy Jensen. Ask for me at security if you change your mind about coming to watch."

She slid her hand into his, shutting her eyes briefly as the erotic rub of work-roughened fingers played havoc with her self-control. She opened her eyes. "I won't."

His shrug was dismissive as he held on to her hand. "And you are?"

Oh Christ. He touched her and she lost her mind. "Oh...sorry. Jocelyn. Garrity. People call me Joss." Why she told him that she had no idea. As if he'd care anyway.

"It's been a pleasure meeting you, *Joss*."

Oh God. That was why. *That was why she'd told him.* She'd wanted to hear it roll off his tongue, all slow and lazy and accented, dragging out that double *s*, somehow making it his own.

She pulled her hand back before she did something really crazy like tug him forward. She knew the way women *knew*, he'd totally be up for a midnight quickie, stranger or not, and her knees went weak.

Sweet baby cheeses. What the hell was wrong with her?

"Good night, Troy. Stay safe this weekend."

He touched the brim of his hat in salute. "Always."

So damn cocky.

AFTER SLEEPING LATE, Troy spent the day checking out the town and the venue for tomorrow night's rodeo. As a veteran of the American Extreme Bull Riders Tour, he'd played much bigger but that's what happened when you got busted down to the pro circuit because you didn't have enough points to compete in the big league.

It was the first time it had happened to him in seven years on the US circuit. He'd taken out the world championship his rookie year, won Barretos in Brazil a couple of years later and won just about every city on the circuit at one time or other. He'd been ranked in the top ten for the last five years. But this last year hadn't been great as his injuries had accumulated and it was the first time he'd been kicked out of the top rankings.

He wasn't worried though. He knew he'd make up the points to rejoin the big league. Winning in Plainview, Big Spring and Lubbock should get him enough points to put him back on the extreme circuit in time for Tucson in August.

And there was something about the feel of the smaller events. He felt closer to the fans, his roots. It reminded him of how it was in the beginning, when he first started out in the circuit back home, sleeping in the back tray of his ute at each event because he couldn't afford a hotel room.

All he'd needed was his swag and the stars and the prospect of riding the meanest, most ornery bulls on offer and he'd been happy as a pig in mud.

Of course, bull riding had given him the means to afford the best hotels but he'd never been interested in the trappings. Or even the money really. It was nice but it didn't mean much when he was living on borrowed time.

He had absolutely no doubt that one day, a one-ton beast was going to get the better of him and a healthy bank balance meant squat when you were dead.

You couldn't take it with you, right?

What he loved more than anything was the camaraderie that came from hanging out with the guys at cheap motels. The smack talk and bullshit. The stories of wild rides and near misses. The celebrations at the end of each night.

And after all that was done? Whatever woman was happy to continue the party privately. And there was never any shortage of them. Bull riding was a high-adrenaline, high-danger sport and that was better than any female Viagra on the market.

Women loved him. Women who, like him, got off on the high of defying death and understood that riding a champion cowboy was a one-night deal.

Not women like Joss Garrity.

Troy took a swig of his beer. He'd been shooting the breeze two doors down with a couple of starry-eyed rookies for the last few hours but it was nine p.m. and everyone was bedding down for the night in preparation for the heats tomorrow. So he was back in his room with just the television, Chinese takeout and his own thoughts for company.

He smiled at the vision of a woman beating the crap out of a set of lug nuts with a wrench. He laughed out loud and shook his head. In all his days, he'd never seen a more magnificent sight, her long ponytail flying, her lips set in a determined line.

Strong too. Her legs evenly spaced, her biceps flexing. He'd half expected to see sparks.

He'd thought about her a lot today. More than had been good for him. In fact she'd been distracting as hell. For someone who thought of women only in relation to the fun he could have with them between the sheets, it puzzled him that instead of thinking about her naked, he'd been replaying that scene from last night.

And hoping like crazy she showed up this weekend.

He reached for his phone—maybe he could track her down? He knew her name, he knew she lived in Plainview and he knew she was a doctor. How hard could it be?

His phone was down to ten percent battery and Troy rose from the small dining table to grab his cable. After searching through his bag he remembered he'd left it in his truck and headed out to retrieve it only to discover the door open and somebody inside it.

"What the fuck?" he bellowed.

The person—male, young, wearing a hoodie—went bug-eyed as Troy descended on the vehicle. He scrambled out of the pickup, just out of Troy's reach, and bolted across the deserted parking lot with Troy in hot pursuit.

He didn't get far. They were evenly matched weight wise but the kid was probably only five eight, to Troy's six foot. Easy enough to crash tackle him to the ground.

"Get off me," the kid yelled, squirming like a fish on a hook, as Troy straddled his back and wrestled with his arms.

"Quit movin'." The kid tried to wriggle out from under him and Troy copped a kick to the ribs. He barely felt it—he'd had worse. "I ride one-ton bulls for a living; you ain't going to buck me off."

After a few more seconds, Troy managed to shackle the kid's hands in his and pull him to his feet. The hoodie had fallen away to reveal a spotty teenager with a scrape on the side of his face where he'd eaten the tar. It was oozing slightly but nothing too deep.

"What in hell were you doing in my car?"

The kid glared belligerently as he tested the strength of the hold Troy had on him. He winced as Troy exerted a little more pressure on his captured wrists. "Looking for money."

Money? Troy understood what it was to be poor. To be on the bones of your ass. To steal to eat. But this kid didn't look like he wanted for anything. His clothes were good; his shoes were decent; he had braces on his teeth for fuck's sake.

"How old are you?"

The boy looked at the ground. "Fifteen."

"You ever heard of a job, mate?"

"Got a job," he mumbled belligerently.

So the kid had no *need* to steal. Was it a bet? A dare? Boredom? Troy also understood stealing for the thrill of it.

For the thrill of getting away with it.

"Do your parents know you're out on the streets?" The

kid continued to stare at his feet, the set to his jaw mutinous. "I take that as a no. Don't you have school tomorrow?"

"Summer vacation." Another mumble.

Of course...Troy had forgotten about summer break. "Not starting out so great for you, huh? How'd you even get here?"

"Bike."

Troy looked around the parking lot, spotting an expensive brand of bicycle leaning against the far hedge. It even had a helmet hanging from the handlebars.

"You're a real badass, huh?"

"You talk dumb."

Troy laughed. The kid needed to work on his insults. "Yeah, well you *are* dumb."

The kid's head snapped up and he glared. "What are you going to do with me?"

"I guess that's up to you." Troy searched the teen's face. Beyond his big talk he was jittery. He didn't have that hard edge, that lack of fear for the consequences that had made Troy such a successful delinquent. He was clearly shitting himself. Which told Troy he had a conscience.

And it wasn't too late for him.

"I can take you to the cops or I can take you to your mother."

"Oh but—"

"Your choice, kid."

Troy cut him off without compunction, noting how he'd

paled at the mention of his mother. The red spots of his acne stood out even more. *Good.* He obviously had a mother and cared about what she thought, which meant she was important to the kid and, judging by appearances, Troy guessed he was important to her as well.

Those kinds of threats hadn't meant squat to Troy. Home had been a nightmare and his parents had been the major cause of his delinquency.

"You want to have the cops ringing your momma to come get you or you want to bypass all that official unpleasantness and have me take you home instead? Either way, mate, she's going to find out."

Troy would know in seconds of meeting the woman whether there was hope for the kid or not. His radar for these kinds of things had been honed through bitter experience.

The kid glared some more but eventually muttered, "Home."

"All right then." Troy gave the kid a shove toward the pickup. "Get in the truck."

THE ONLY CONVERSATION that passed between Troy and the kid for fifteen minutes were directions. Troy figured he was too busy framing excuses for his mother to chat. And letting the kid stew for a while in the quagmire of potential punishments and possibly, his crap-filled underwear, was penalty itself.

"It's this one."

Troy pulled up outside a very middle-class-looking suburban house. It wasn't anything flashy but it was a decent-sized house on a big block, with a picket fence, a neatly trimmed path, a small front porch and a driveway that ran down the side to an A-framed building he assumed was the garage. He'd have killed to have had this growing up.

He cut the engine and undid his seat belt.

The kid threw a startled glance his way. "You don't need to come in."

Troy laughed. "Nice try, kid." Obviously he'd been planning on not saying anything at all to his mother about the *incident.*

His gaze darted from Troy to his front door and back to Troy again. "She won't be home for ages."

"No worries." Troy opened his door. "I can wait."

The kid didn't move to unbuckle his belt—he just sat in the passenger seat staring through the window at his house, a picture of misery. It was Troy who opened his door. "Come on, dude. Best just to get it over with."

He felt sorry for the kid in a way. How many times had Troy wished that someone would cut him a break when he'd been in trouble, usually in the back seat of a cop car? It had happened eventually. Not in the way he'd hoped or that he'd even appreciated at the time but his fork in the road had come.

Tonight was this kid's fork in the road. He wasn't playing in the same ballpark Troy had played in but delinquency was a rocky slope.

The teen sighed and undid his belt and for a brief moment Troy caught a glassy shimmer in the kid's eyes before he pushed rudely past and headed for the house. Troy followed behind, slowing as the kid's pace slowed the closer they got to the door. He took the two steps to the porch and stood in front of the door like it was the gallows.

Troy drew up beside him. "Key?"

The kid stared straight ahead. "Nope."

So, it was going to be the hard way. For the person on the other side as well when they opened the door to find their guilty-looking son and the stranger he'd tried to rob. Troy lifted his hand and knocked, two quick raps against the solid wood.

Footsteps could be heard almost immediately and the kid shifted uneasily beside him. The porch light flicked on, illuminating the kid's guilt tenfold. There was the sound of a dead bolt releasing then the door swung open.

Troy blinked at the woman standing there. He remembered that ponytail from last night. And the generous mouth and how it balanced out her pointy chin and cute chipmunk cheeks.

He hadn't been able to make out the color of her eyes though. Until now. Gray.

"Joss?"

The kid's head turned, a frown crinkling his brow as he stared at Troy.

"Troy?" She looked at the kid, at the scrape on his face. "Damien?" She reached out to touch it but he pulled away. She glanced at Troy again then back to her son.

This kid—*Damien*—this sullen, really crap thief was Joss-from-last-night's son? Joss who'd given him a hard-on just from her unorthodox use of a lug wrench.

She was a *mother*? She hadn't been wearing a ring last night, or tonight either. And she hadn't thrown a husband in his face when he'd flirted.

Troy performed a quick calculation in his head. Joss must have been nineteen when she'd had him.

"Damien?" she repeated, looking him up and down as if searching for other injuries. "What happened? You went to bed over an hour ago." She glanced at Troy again. "What's going on here?"

"*You're* his mother?"

"Yes."

What. The. Actual. Fuck.

Troy was speechless. If this wasn't the world's biggest coincidence he didn't know what was. If he was a religious man he might have fallen to his knees and praised Jesus. But now wasn't the time to get religion.

Now he had to go ahead and break the woman's heart.

Troy cocked an eyebrow at Damien. "You want to tell

her or you want me to?"

"Tell me what?" she demanded, her ponytail swishing as she continued to glance between the two of them. "Damien? Oh God...what have you done now?"

Now? Interesting... This obviously wasn't the first time the kid—Damien—had been in trouble. Damien shoved his hands into the front pockets of his hoodie and dropped his gaze.

Troy sighed. "I caught him ransacking my car. For money."

Her gasp was loud enough to be heard in New Mexico. "*Damien William Garrity!*" Her fiery hiss and demonic glare even scared Troy a little bit. "Is that true?"

Damien couldn't even look at his mother. Man, he sucked at this. Troy hoped he was getting a good education because he was not going to be able to pull off a life of crime. Guilt poured off him in visible waves.

"How *could* you?" she demanded, grabbing his arms and giving him a shake, despite the kid being bigger and taller. "You're a *thief* now? Are you freaking kidding me?" She shook him again. "I didn't leave Chicago for you to become some two-bit hoodlum in *Texas*, do you understand? *You want to go to jail?* Because that's what happens to thieves."

Not if they don't get caught. God knew for every time Troy had been caught, there'd been nine times he hadn't.

She dropped her hands. "What do you think your dad would say about this? You think he'd be proud of you now?"

Troy winced internally at the well-aimed guilt trip. *So, there was a dad.* He noticed a tear roll down Damien's cheek and felt absurdly like putting his arm around the kid.

"*Do you?*" she yelled.

"No, ma'am." Damien's voice cracked.

Her expression softened for a moment and Troy thought he saw a shimmer of moisture in her eyes caught by the porch light before her features hardened again. "Apologize to Mr. Jensen."

"I'm sorry," Damien mumbled at the ground.

"Look. At. Him," she barked. "And mean it!"

Damien raised a miserable face, two wet tracks glistening down his cheeks. He looked Troy directly in the eye. "I'm sorry, Mr. Jensen, for breaking into your truck."

His voice was clear if a little shaky, the apology sincere.

"Thank you," his mother snapped, her fists clenching and unclenching by her sides. "Right. You're grounded. *Indefinitely.* That's going to suck for summer vacation, isn't it?"

The kid didn't protest. So perhaps he wasn't as dumb as Troy had thought.

"Go to your room. I'll be in to clean up your face after I discuss what extra punishment Mr. Jensen would like to see meted out."

Damien didn't need to be asked twice. He hightailed it into the house faster than a thrown cowboy gets up off the dirt. They both watched him retreat until a door slammed somewhere inside the house and she turned back to face him.

Her big gray eyes looked tired. And sad.

"I'm so, *so* sorry…"

She drew in a ragged breath and wrapped her arms around her middle, which emphasized very nice breasts beneath her navy tank top. No bra.

"I perfectly understand if you want to get the police involved."

Troy blinked. Now *that* he hadn't expected. She hadn't tried to feed him a bunch of BS excuses or blame her son's actions on anyone else. She'd accepted responsibility and made him do likewise. And he admired the hell out of her for it.

It was the kind of discipline and lesson in consequences his parents hadn't cared enough to give.

Nobody had given a shit about him.

Chapter Three

TROY SHOOK HIS head. "That won't be necessary."

She visibly sagged before his eyes, shooting him a grateful smile. "How much did he take? I'll repay you."

"I caught him before he took anything."

"I…don't know what to do with him." Her voice was wobbly, her eyes glassy. "I'm at my wits' end."

She cocked her hip, leaning against the doorframe, crossing one bare ankle over the other. She was in loose shorts that fell to mid thigh showing off solidly muscled legs.

Strong legs.

The kind of legs that could squeeze a horse or a bull or hell, a man for that matter, taking him in whatever direction she wanted. He'd always been a girls-in-skinny-jeans kinda guy but those legs were causing him to rethink long-held beliefs.

They conjured up images of her riding him. *All. Night. Long.* Which was hardly appropriate to be thinking about right now.

"His father?"

She shook her head. "Died five years ago."

Troy's gut tightened. He barely knew Joss or her son but he knew enough about crap fathers to understand the importance of *good* ones. He only had to look at how Joss had been able to bring Damien to tears just mentioning his father to know her dead husband had been one of the good ones.

"I'm sorry."

"It's fine. It seems like a whole other lifetime ago sometimes."

Maybe. But her voice had softened and Troy didn't need to be a psychologist to catch the wistfulness in her tone. He wondered if her husband's death had anything to do with their move from Chicago.

"I just wish I knew what he was thinking, you know?" Her eyebrows knotted as she searched his face for who knew what.

"You're a guy. Can you shed any light on what the hell goes through a teenage boy's head?"

Troy was pretty sure she *did not* want to know the kind of things that occupied the brain of a fifteen-year-old male. There was some stuff mothers just *shouldn't* know. "Well that would be breaking the guy code," he teased. "Suffice to say that most of it involves chicks and heavy levels of nudity."

"Oh God…" She groaned. "Don't. I'm not ready for that. I don't even want to *think* about it."

He laughed. "Stealing doesn't look so bad now, does it?"

She groaned again. "They both suck."

"Well if it's any consolation, I don't think he's going to be stealing again anytime soon."

"Yeah, but how often *has* he been doing it?"

She chewed on her bottom lip and Troy lost his place in the conversation. He wanted to step right up into her space, slide his hand onto her waist and soothe that bottom lip with his tongue.

His dick got hard at the thought but he was pretty sure she'd knee him in the balls if he even attempted such a move.

Unfortunately, not even the prospect of that killed his erection.

"I mean how often has he already been out wandering the streets at night when I thought he was in bed?"

Troy shrugged, grateful for the rhetorical question as he dragged his thoughts off her mouth.

"Where did it happen?" she asked. "At the arena?"

"No." He shook his head. "At the Motel 6 where I'm staying."

"*What?*" She straightened. Troy did his best not to ogle the corresponding jiggle of her breasts. "That's on the outskirts of town! How on earth did he get out there?"

He hooked his thumb over his shoulder. "Bike."

She stared at the bicycle Troy had stowed in the back of his truck. "*What the—*"

She stopped abruptly and Troy got the distinct impression she'd been about to say fuck. What the *fuck*. The thought of such a dirty word coming out of that pretty mouth didn't really help the situation in his pants.

"Right." She narrowed her eyes at the bicycle. "I know *exactly* how that kid is getting punished. No bike for the entire summer. He wants to run around Plainview like some kind of gangster then he can do it on his feet."

Troy chuckled. He probably shouldn't have but she was pretty magnificent vibrating with annoyance and vengeance, her ponytail swishing with each angry word. "I'm sorry." He held up his hands in surrender as she glared at him. "It's not funny."

She glared some more before a slow, grudging smile puffed up her chipmunk cheeks. "Sorry." She dropped her head against the doorframe. "But that kid…" She took a deep breath and let it out. "Don't ever have kids, Troy—they become teenagers whose sole purpose in life is to piss you off."

More dirty words. *Heaven help him.* "Bulls aren't much better."

She snorted. "I think I'd rather face down a raging bull than Damien at the moment."

Troy laughed. "I'd pay good money to see that."

Her breath hitched as their gazes met and held. Her eyes widened slightly and damn if her cheeks didn't warm up right before his eyes. Her hand crept up to her chest, her fingers coming to rest lightly around the base of her throat.

She was the one to break the growing silence.

"God…I'm sorry." Her hand slid from her throat to absently pat her chest just above her cleavage. It drew his gaze to the two hard points of her nipples, tenting the fabric of her top.

His erection went from hard to granite.

"Would you like to come in for a coffee? Or a drink?" she added hastily. "It's the least I can offer you after what Damien did. I'm sure I have some hard liquor around here somewhere. Gus likes a slug every now and then."

Troy tensed. "Gus?" There was *another* guy?

"Damien's grandfather. My father-in-law. We live with him."

Ah. Troy relaxed.

"Did you want to come in?"

The only *hard liquor* Troy was interested in right now had nothing to do with booze and everything to do with burying his head between those strong thighs of hers. And even he wasn't crass enough to press his luck with a woman who was worried her son was turning into a *gangster.*

While said son was in the house.

Not to mention her dead husband's father.

Joss was complicated. And Troy didn't do complicated. He sure as hell didn't play with single mothers. He may have been a total horn dog but even he knew a guy didn't mess with that dynamic.

No matter how well Joss hit a lug nut. Or how strong her thighs. Or how hard his dick.

"No, it's okay. But thank you." He smiled. "I probably

should be hitting the sack. Big night tomorrow night."

"Okay…sure." Was that disappointment in her voice? She pushed off the doorframe. "Thank you. *Again.*" She shook her head. "I seem to be always thanking you."

He shrugged. "As I said last night, my pleasure." Her teeth dug into her bottom lip again and Troy shoved his hands into his back pockets. Just in case. "Maybe I'll see you around?"

"As long as it's not in my ER."

"Amen to that."

Troy laughed and she joined him, her breasts bouncing enticingly. Hell if he didn't want to tug up the hem of her shirt and put his mouth to them. Right here on her doorstep with the porch light spotlighting them for the whole neighborhood to see.

"Well…good night then." If he didn't leave now he might just follow through on that impulse and he had no desire to feel that strong thigh smashing into his testicles. "You want me to keep the bike for a few days? Let your son think you got rid of it?"

She smiled and it drew his gaze to her mouth. Like he didn't want to kiss her badly enough already. "Devious," she murmured. "I like the way you think."

"It's not even my best quality."

"Oh yeah? What *is* your best quality?"

Troy's breath heated in his lungs at the tease in her voice. "Come watch me on the weekend."

"Your best quality is how you ride a bull?"

"Nope." Troy shook his head slow and deliberate. "It's what I do with all that adrenaline afterward."

It was satisfying to see the cool, clear gray of her eyes shimmer and liquefy and to hear her long husky exhalation. He figured a doctor would know *all* the ways to deal with an adrenaline high.

"Night, Joss."

He smiled as he turned away and headed for his truck, his heart pounding, his erection raging.

TROY ZONED OUT the buzz of the crowd in the packed arena as he centered himself, focusing on the thick thud of his pulse bounding through his chest, his abdomen, his groin. Everything melted away—the boom of the announcer over the speakers, the guys around him in the chute and the powerful shift of an angry bull between his legs.

It was just him and his heartbeat.

The pound of blood, the rush of oxygen, the wash of adrenaline.

"You ready?"

Troy tightened his grip on his rope and raised his left hand in the air. He nodded. "Go."

With a clatter and a roar from the crowd, the chute flew open and Troy was pitched forward as his mean-ass bull—

Gandalf—bucked right out of the gate.

Yes, you sonofabitch, that's right. Buck me off. I dare you.

The announcer whipped the crowd up as the bull kicked and spun, twisting its massive sixteen hundred pound weight in the air, doing its level best to throw its unwanted burden into the dirt.

Troy was tall for a bull rider. And lanky. Mostly they were shorter, stockier guys with a lower center of gravity. But he'd learned to compensate early with extraordinary upper body flexibility and almost innate instincts for which way a bull was going to turn. He was also better than just about anyone in the business in using his raised hand for counterbalance.

"You're mine, Gandalf," he taunted, enjoying the thrill as his body jerked back and forth.

Troy squeezed his thighs tight against the dun-colored hide as the bull threatened to pull his roped arm out of its socket with every jarring drop. All he had to do tonight to take out the comp and earn precious points was to stay for eight lousy seconds.

Eight seconds that felt like eight hundred as Gandalf kicked and bucked and dropped. Troy's pulse washed like Niagara Falls through his ears as he counted off the seconds in his head, waiting for the buzzer.

One. Two. Three. Gandalf twisted violently to the right. Troy sensed it coming but still his pulse spiked as he slewed sideways. He lost his hat before righting himself.

Four. Five. Six. The bull kicked out his back legs and dropped with bone-jarring suddenness onto his front.

Seven...Eight!

The buzzer blared; the crowd went wild. He threw back his head and hollered at the top of his lungs. A rush of invincibility flooded his system. He was bulletproof. He was fucking *indestructible*.

He was king of the world.

Gandalf did not agree, the bull bucking him off before he had a chance to dismount. Troy sailed through the air, hitting the ground *hard,* his bent left arm taking the full impact.

His vision grayed as white-hot pain sliced up and down his arm, movement impossible. He lay facedown inhaling dirt through clenched teeth, waiting for the crunch of his skull under the hard smack of Gandalf's hooves.

But the clowns rushed the bull, distracting him from venting his fury on the rider who dared defy him. The Wonder from Down Under had taken out the top prize.

But his elbow paid the price.

TROY DIDN'T REMEMBER a whole lot after that. A haze of pain disconnected his brain and then a wonderful hit of who-the-hell-cared-what plunged him into a rainbow and out the other side.

Troy had suffered many an injury. Shoulders, knees, ankles. Bruises, lacerations, broken bones. Tendons, ligaments, organs. So it wasn't his first brush with narcotics. But it *was* the best.

Thousands of tiny fingers stroked every millimeter of his skin.

Every millimeter.

There was pleasure and swirling lights. Everything was pretty and glowing. The whole first sixteen years of his life were erased and the memory of every orgasm he'd ever been the grateful recipient of whispered sweet nothings against his sensitized skin.

He floated in a warm pool of bliss while the pain in his arm was a vague dull ache somewhere out of reach.

No wonder his parents had been hooked on drugs. Why spend time in their shitty dysfunctional lives taking care of him when they could feel this damn good?

"Troy."

Joss. He smiled as her voice took the place of the fingers, making delicious promises as it massaged his body.

"Troy!" She gave his uninjured arm a hard shake. "It's Joss Garrity. Wake up."

He smiled again, forcing open eyes that felt super-glued together. "You again," he said dreamily as she came into soft focus, all big gray eyes and chipmunk cheeks. A ponytail long enough to wrap around his hand several times.

She was in a navy scrub top with some white blurry

stitching on the pocket, a stethoscope slung around her neck.

"You're glowing, like an angel. With a ponytail."

He laughed at his own humor. An angel with a ponytail seemed *hysterically* funny.

"*Ooo*kay. No more morphine for you."

"Whatever you say, doc." Troy didn't mind. His eyes drifted shut. Absolutely nothing bothered him at the moment.

"*Troy!*" A harder shake this time.

"Hmm, bossy," he murmured, coordinating his eyelids better this time. They opened faster if not all the way. "I like that."

"You've dislocated your elbow."

"Not me." He shook his head. "Gandalf did it."

"Okay." She nodded and her ponytail bounced. "*Definitely* no more morphine for you."

"Oh no, ma'am…that was the name of the bull."

Troy rolled his head to the side to locate who'd spoken. "Hey, Diego! *Dude.*" The rookie grasped Troy's good arm. One of the medical team from the rodeo was also in the cubicle.

"You won, man."

Troy laughed. It floated somewhere above his head. "Course I did. I'm the Wonder from Down Under."

A light, tinkly laugh carried from somewhere down near his feet, penetrating his bubble. He shifted his focus with difficulty. A pretty, skinny blonde smiled at him. He smiled back out of politeness and habit. But she didn't hold a candle to Joss.

Joss. God. Even her name turned him on.

He dragged his gaze away, trying to locate her with eyes that didn't want to focus. "You're beautiful, you know that?" He reached for her ponytail but his arm weighed a ton and it fell uselessly to the trolley.

He thought he heard a snigger coming from Diego's direction but Joss didn't pass any comment—she just plowed on. "We need to get an X-ray to be certain but I'm pretty sure it'll confirm my suspicions. As soon as they are, we'll need to pop the joint back into place."

"Pop!" He shoved his index finger into the side of his cheek and it made a loud popping sound as he forced it out. He laughed. "Simple as that."

"Well…it's probably going to hurt a bit."

Troy smiled at her with all the joy and pleasure that was floating round inside him. "Honey, I'm not feeling *any* pain at the moment."

Her hand fell to his shoulder and she patted him. "Trust me. You will."

HALF AN HOUR later, Troy was still drifting along in a lovely drug haze, still feeling no pain, when Joss grasped his forearm and told him to take some deep breaths. The nurse with the laugh held his upper arm firmly with both of her hands.

"It'll be quick, but it'll hurt like the blazes as it slips back in. Are you ready?"

Troy waved his good hand airily in a dismissive gesture. "I get bucked off bulls for a living. I can handle a few seconds of pain."

"Okay." She took a deep breath. "Here goes."

The procedure took about twenty seconds and Troy felt only a vague kind of pressure until the last two seconds when it felt like she was amputating his arm through the elbow joint with a blunt, rusty knife.

"*Fuuuck!*" he swore loud enough for everyone in the emergency department to hear him as he jackknifed into a sitting position, his heart rate and blood pressure spiking into the stroke zone.

Had he been in his right mind he'd have apologized for his language. But he was in a world of agony.

It hurt far worse than the actual dislocation had. But as quickly as the pain erupted, it dissipated, evaporating in the same blinding flash it had arrived, and he collapsed back against the thin mattress, with a grunt.

"There." She nodded and patted his chest again. "Good as new."

"Christ." Troy took a deep, shuddery breath. "Remind me not to get into an arm wrestle with you."

Then he closed his eyes and headed back into the rainbow.

Chapter Four

Two hours later, Joss checked back in on her patient. She was knocking off soon and she thought she'd discharge him before she left for the night. There really was no need for him to stay. He'd had another X-ray, which had shown pleasing relocation, there were no fractures that would require orthopedic follow-up, his neurovascular observations had checked out and a splint had been applied.

She twitched the cubicle curtain back. He was alone, flaked out on the gurney, the young cowboy and the medic from the rodeo having departed a while ago leaving Troy to sleep it off. Her gaze was drawn automatically to his long, lean form, his dusty boots hanging over the end of the trolley. Just-as-dusty fringed chaps encased his jeans except for the area over his crotch, which accentuated the bulge there like a bloody great bull's-eye.

As if his big-ass belt buckle didn't already draw the gaze to that part of his anatomy.

"Hippocratic oath, Joss," she whispered.

Her gaze wandered higher. They'd relieved him of his shirt earlier and he was still shirtless. The splint he'd been put into bent his arm at ninety degrees so it rested across his stomach but that still left an awful lot of smooth, hard, honed, golden skin exposed.

Higher still, his jaw was dusted with dark growth, his mouth was slack in slumber and that tiny white scar in his eyebrow was fascinating as all giddy up. His close-cropped hair revealed a beautifully symmetric skull in stark contrast to his crooked nose.

Basically he was a young, fit, hot guy—a *cowboy* no less—who was a sheer pleasure to look at and she had no right to be ogling him like he was a piece of meat.

But damn the universe for throwing him at her. *Three times.*

What the hell was she supposed to make of that?

Joss approached the gurney, resting a hand on the railing. She fixed her gaze on his face, not his body and took a moment to gather herself. "Troy." He didn't stir and she cleared her throat of its ridiculous breathiness. "*Troy.*"

It was louder and had the desired effect, which saved her from having to touch him. Probably wise to avoid that at all costs.

He opened his eyes, his brow furrowing as he looked at her, the dreamy smile from earlier gone. He lifted his head to look at his arm, then around him before returning his gaze to lock on her.

Green. His eyes were green. She'd been in too much of a state to compute that on Thursday night.

"Hey," she said quietly as he finally seemed to focus. "I thought you weren't going to end up in my ER?"

"What can I say?" He flopped his head back against the mattress. "I wanted to see you again."

Joss laughed, ignoring the flutter of her pulse at his easy flirting. The man *obviously* didn't know how to turn it off. "How are you feeling? You dislocated your elbow, remember?"

He glanced at his splinted arm again. "Vaguely."

Joss smiled. "Yeah. You've been a little out of it. We give good drugs around here."

"Oh God." He shut his eyes briefly before they flicked open again. "I wasn't an asshole, was I?"

"On the contrary. You were pretty funny. Morphine agrees with you." He grimaced, clearly not happy at the pronouncement. "How's the pain?"

He lifted his arm experimentally. "Feels okay. I've had worse."

"That'll be the residual narcotic. It'll probably be more painful in the morning from stretched ligaments and inflammation. I'll send you home with some painkillers just in case."

"How long does the splint have to be on for?"

"At least two weeks, maybe three. Depends on how diligent you are with your physical therapy."

"Yeah." He frowned. "That's not going to work."

Joss cocked an eyebrow at the flinty tone in his voice.

Nothing lazy about it now. "Oh?"

"I have Big Spring next weekend. And Lubbock two weeks after that."

"Yeah." She smiled sweetly. "That's not going to work."

"I have to compete." His mouth set in a grim line. "I need the points if I want to get back into the extreme tour. Got to be in Tucson in August."

"You can maybe make Lubbock. But next week? Sorry...you take another fall and land on your arm again?" She shook her head. "It's much more susceptible to repeat dislocation now especially in these next few weeks and you could do permanent damage if it happens again. Hell, you may not even be able to straighten your arm properly from this dislocation."

"*What?*" He half sat before grimacing and slumping back.

"It's possible that you could have reduced range of movement. Extension problems aren't uncommon after elbow dislocation."

He shook his head, his jaw set. "That's not acceptable."

Joss sighed. Whether it was acceptable or not it was a cold hard fact. It never ceased to amaze her how many jocks and professional sportsmen who relied on their body for their living weren't prepared to give it the proper time to heal when it was injured.

It didn't make sense.

"Well do your physical therapy like a good boy, take

your painkillers, stay off bulls and have some patience." She folded her arms. "Now, how are you getting back to the motel?"

He looked like he was going to argue some more, shifting slowly in the gurney to a more upright position but something pulled him up short and he winced. "I'll catch a cab."

"And is there someone who can keep an eye on you?" He'd been pretty wiped out from the morphine. She'd be more comfortable discharging him if she was doing it to someone's care.

"Are you kidding? The rodeo's over. The motel will be full of yahooing bull riders."

"I mean someone who'll actually look in on you, not be drunk off their ass while you throw up in your sleep and choke on your own vomit."

He cocked an eyebrow at her. "I bet you're fun at parties."

Parties? Ha! She should be so lucky. "I'm a real treat."

"Well you've no need to worry about me vomiting in my sleep. I have no plans to hit the sack, not when there are celebrations going on."

"I'd advise against that. Sleep is what you need."

He snorted. "You think I'm going to be able to sleep with a bunch of cowboys drinking and playing country music in the parking lot until the sun comes up? Besides, I could really murder a beer right about now."

Joss crossed her arms. *Sweet baby cheeses.* This was going

from bad to worse. "For starters, you should lay off the alcohol while you're taking painkillers. And secondly, I'd recommend a couple of *quiet* days with your arm. You get drunk on top of your morphine and start waving that thing around like you're bulletproof or God forbid fall over on it and it'll make things worse. You need to rest it so it's not too sore to start physical therapy in a couple of days."

"Relax, doc. I promise not to get shitfaced, okay? And I'm used to pushing through the pain during physical therapy. I kick PT ass. Ask anybody."

Relax. God, he reminded her so much of Damien. Relax, Mom. Chill. Stop making a fuss. Everything's cool. Except he was heading toward delinquency and she didn't know what in hell to do about it.

And *pushing through the pain* was plain old dumb.

"I liked you better when you were drugged."

"Yeah well, I liked you better when I was drugged too."

He grabbed the railing of the gurney and gingerly pulled himself up into a sitting position. Picking up his splinted arm, he tucked it in closer to his torso. A sudden sheet of pallor swept over his face and he swayed for a second or two.

"Troy?" She reached for his shoulder at the same time he grabbed the railing. His skin was warm and firm beneath hers, the roundness of his shoulder joint filling her palm.

"Are you okay?"

"Just a little dizzy. Sat up too fast." He blinked and shook his head as if to clear it. "I'm good now. Can I go?"

For the love of Mike. *This guy.*

His dizziness probably was only postural and she couldn't justify keeping him here. He'd no doubt refuse anyway if that mulish set to his jaw was anything to go by but she'd be an idiot to discharge him to a booze-fueled party where he could potentially injure himself further hanging around a bunch of hopped-up cowboys.

"Why don't I just admit you for the night?"

"To the hospital?" He stared at her incredulously. "No way." He rattled the rail, narrowing his eyes to green slits. "Let me out, doc."

Joss stood her ground. "I don't think going back to the motel is a good idea."

He rolled his eyes. "Okay. I'll sleep in the back of my pickup—it's still at the arena."

Was he crazy? Why on earth would he think *that* was a more palatable option? She shook her head. "*Absolutely* not."

"Then I'll find a buckle bunny to tend to me through the night. I'm sure there'll be a few of them at the party."

Joss blinked. "A *what?*"

"You know, like a groupie. A rodeo groupie."

"You call them *buckle bunnies?*" The term was crass and degrading and made her wince.

"Hell no." He held up his un-splinted hand in a surrender motion. "They call themselves that. With pride. And I don't see anything wrong with women who are up front about what they want from you. They're out to bag some cowboys, maybe grab a buckle or two as a trophy. That's honesty."

Joss couldn't decide if her feminist principles were insulted or whether she was just plain jealous of such sexual liberation. "And I bet you're real popular with the…" It was no use—she couldn't say it. "Them. Right?"

"Well, I'm not a virgin, if that's what you're asking."

Joss scowled at him, his answer rubbing her the wrong way. The fact they'd somehow veered off track even more so. How many women he'd slept with was none of her business.

"And the likelihood of you resting that arm if you found a…friend for the night?"

He grinned. "Not high."

"So…we're back to square one."

"Well hell, *Joss*, unless you're offering to take me home to yours, I'm shit out of options."

"Okay fine, come back to my place."

She didn't know who was more stunned by her offer. Her. Or him. She knew he hadn't actually meant it but faced with the choices it was a good solution. At least that's what she told herself because the thought that it may have been the way he'd said her name—with a slight burr of exasperation to it—was too confusing to consider.

And anyway, it was the least she could do for the man who had stopped and helped her in her hour of need on Wednesday night. *And* brought her thieving son home the next night without making an unholy ruckus over it.

This was Troy's hour of need—whether the idiot realized it or not. It was her turn to help him.

And it was just one night.

"Really?" He eased himself back onto the mattress, his lazy grin from Wednesday night back in full force. "I'm not sure I'll be up to much but…" He shrugged. "If you're willing to get on top."

"I have a couch." Joss hoped like hell her sarcastic smile masked the sudden flurry of images in her head all involving her in nothing but that big-ass belt buckle, *riding* him like her own personal cowboy. "It's possibly the most uncomfortable piece of furniture in the entire existence of the world but you're young; you'll cope."

"Way to talk it up, doc."

Joss ignored him, unlatching the rail and easing it down. "Let's go." She grabbed the brown paper bag stowed under the trolley with his shirt and hat in it, conscious of him lying there unmoving, watching her. "You need some help?"

She hoped not. She really hoped not. Acres of golden tanned skin were tempting enough without having to lay her hands on it.

"Nah." He smiled again. "I'm good."

He sat then in one smooth easy action, his abdominals bunching as he swung his legs over the side of the gurney. Joss waited a beat or two in case he lost his color and swayed again. "Dizzy?"

"Nope."

Satisfied he was telling the truth she opened the clothing bag. "You want to put your shirt on?"

Please, please, want to put your shirt on.

He shook his head, his green eyes holding hers. "I'm fine."

Oh yes he was. Very, *very* fine.

"All right then." Joss stood aside for him. "Let's get the paperwork sorted and we'll go."

His body crowded hers briefly as he slid from the gurney and she took a step back but not before his heat and aroma surrounded her. She'd expected him to smell like a farmyard. Like dirt and cattle. But he smelled like leather and rope.

And didn't that do strange things to her pulse.

"You hungry?" he asked as they passed a vending machine.

"Not really."

Not for anything that was in a vending machine anyway. Joss clenched her hands by her sides as he headed toward the machine, his bare, smooth back utterly lickable. It made her want things she hadn't thought about in a very long time.

Like her nails marks down all its lean golden perfection.

As soon as Joss started the car Troy was out like a light, obviously still suffering from the effects of injury and heavy-duty narcotics. He'd slammed down a can of Mountain Dew and a packet of Cheetos while he'd waited for her and now here he was, sleeping like a baby.

So much for wanting to party the rest of the night.

Having him in the close confines of her car was an exercise in self-control she wasn't sure she was going to win.

Wasn't sure she wanted to with his eyelashes casting ridiculously long shadows on his cheeks whenever a streetlight flashed by and she saw his lips still coated in Cheeto dust.

Reminding herself she was a doctor and he was her patient didn't help. Because technically he wasn't her patient. Not anymore. Which only made her feel marginally better about the sudden flashes of lust that gripped her every time the streetlights sliced in through the windshield, illuminating the flat perfection of his abs.

Andy had owned a nice set of abs. She'd forgotten how much she'd loved to look at them, to touch them.

Thankfully home was only a six-minute drive and she didn't have to put up with the double temptation of abs and Cheeto lips for too long.

He stirred when she cut the engine in the garage, his face screwing tight at the movement.

"Starting to hurt?"

"A little." He winced as he reached for the door handle but pushed on without complaint, following her into the kitchen via the back door.

The house was silent. It was close to eleven and both Damien and Gus would be dead to the world but it didn't stop her tiptoeing in, relying on the moonlight flooding in through the windows rather than electricity to move past the dining table and whispering, "Follow me."

It had been five years since Andy died and this had never been *their* house. But it had been his childhood home and it felt weird bringing another man into it. Not to mention it *was* Andy's father's house. How would he feel about it?

She walked from the kitchen across a hallway into the massive sunken living room that faced the street. Large picture windows let in ambient light from out front allowing her to easily navigate to the couch.

"This is it." She kept her voice low as she turned to face him and almost took a step back when she realized how close he was. Leather and rope oozed in the space between them.

He looked down his body. "I'm kinda dusty," he said, his voice also low.

Joss refused to follow his gaze, fixing hers instead on the way light from outside fell on the naked slopes of his shoulders. "It's seen worse. I'll just get you some sheets."

"No need. This is luxurious compared to a lot of the paces I've bunked down."

"I'll get a blanket. It might be summer but the nights can still cool down."

She turned to leave but he grabbed her arm gently and she stilled. "I won't need it. I don't get cold."

She believed him. The imprint of his hand burned right through her clothes and she remembered how Andy had always felt like an oven. She missed that about sleeping with a man. How toasty warm they were.

Sweet baby cheeses. She was in trouble.

She shook his hand loose, delved in her bag for the bottle of painkillers and placed them on the nearby coffee table with a rattle. "I'll just get you some water."

She ignored his whispered protest, forging on to the kitchen. Her hand trembled as she turned on the faucet and filled a glass, her heartbeat tripping crazily against her pulse points.

This was madness. What the hell was wrong with her? Her body had taken on a life of its own. "Pull yourself together, Joss," she lectured under her breath, giving the faucet an extra vicious twist as she turned it off.

Chapter Five

H E WAS SITTING on the couch when Joss returned. He'd removed his boots but was muttering curses at the pill bottle he'd crammed between his abs and the splint. He was clearly having problems negotiating the safety cap one-handed.

"Let me." She placed the glass on the coffee table and grabbed the bottle out of his unresisting grasp. "How bad is it?"

He slumped against the couch, the back of his head dropping along the rolled cushioned top, his eyes shutting. "Hurts like a bitch."

Joss unscrewed the bottle and decanted two pills. "Here."

He reached out blindly for the pills, his fingertips grazing her flesh. Goose bumps fanned up her arm, crept up her nape and buzzed her hairline. He tossed the pills back, his eyes still shut, his throat bobbing as he swallowed.

Joss picked up the water and stepped closer, nudging his knee with hers. "Wash them down with this."

He roused, levering himself forward, his legs spread wide in a very male way. He took the glass and drank, draining it before handing it back. Their fingers brushed, which did strange things to her equilibrium.

"Thank you." His voice was a rough whisper, his face upturned as he dropped his hand to his thigh. "For the water. For patching me up." He smiled. "For the drugs."

Joss smiled too, the quiet of the night and their voices creating a strange intimacy.

"And for bringing me back to your place."

She was achingly aware of how close they were. Aware of the hairsbreadth distance separating their legs. Aware of how her body towered over his. Aware of his spread thighs and the opening in his chaps spotlighting his crotch.

Aware of his potency.

She was about to take a step back when his hand slid onto her leg. Slow and lazy.

"You don't wear your scrubs home," he murmured, his fingers idly stroking just behind her knee, the denim of her jeans no barrier to the sensations sweeping up her leg.

Joss willed herself to move but not one damn synapse obeyed. It was as if his fingers had injected them with a paralyzing agent.

"No." Her voice was hushed yet high. Breathy. "It's against hospital policy."

"Pity." He smiled at her. "You look hot in them."

If it was possible to orgasm through compliments alone, she'd just moved into the red zone. He was dangerously good for her ego.

His hand moved higher, applying subtle pressure. Joss swayed closer, somehow finding herself standing between his thighs, his fingers fanning inexorably north, creating all kinds of havoc. Sensation streaked to her inner thighs and tingled hot and urgent between her legs. The air was so thick in her lungs she was barely breathing.

The urge to place her hands on his shoulders, to push him back, to slide her thighs either side of his and straddle him...

Sweet baby cheeses.

It had been a long time since she'd had a man between her legs.

His palm came to rest where the groove of her thigh met her ass. "I bet you look hot out of them too." The hoarse whisper combined with the illicit nature of the moment brushed like sandpaper over her skin. "With just a stethoscope around your neck. And my belt buckle."

The startling accuracy of his fantasy, so closely aligned to her earlier one, was exactly what she needed.

The proverbial bucket of cold water.

She stepped back almost tripping over the coffee table in her haste. What the hell was she doing?

What the hell was *he* doing?

She righted herself, scrambling around the other side of the table. But not even the heavy mahogany felt sufficient protection from the hormonal juju he was pumping out.

"*Don't.*" Her voice was shaky, her cheeks aflame.

Once again he held up his good hand in surrender. "Okay."

"This is *not* happening between us."

He shrugged, slow and lazy. "Okay."

Joss was not comforted by his response. It was hardly groveling capitulation. Not that she wanted him on his knees in front of her.

No. She absolutely, *positively*, did not want that.

She narrowed her eyes. "I mean it."

"I believe you."

Which wasn't exactly comforting either. But if being a mother had taught her anything it had taught her retreat was sometimes the wisest course of action.

Time to get the hell out of Dodge.

"Good night."

He touched his forehead in mock salute and she turned away before he could add anything more. Not that it stopped him. "Sweet dreams," he whispered.

It followed her all the way to her bed.

JOSS WAS STILL lying awake two hours later. Frankly she was terrified of falling asleep in case those dreams turned out to be far from sweet. Troy on the other hand was sleeping like a baby, stretched out half naked and dusty on her couch.

She'd checked on him an hour ago—purely from a medical standpoint—and man, had that had been a mistake. Even asleep his presence dominated, his good arm thrust above his head, his face turned toward it, his damn crooked nose pressed into his damn perfect bicep.

The foot closest to the edge of the couch was flat on the floor spreading his thighs wide. His jeans rode low on his hips, his buckle giving off a dull shine in the ambient light, drawing her attention north to his belly button and south to that bull's-eye between his legs.

And here she was, lying in bed thinking about that target. Thinking about every delectable inch of him. Feeling like a horny teenager one moment and a dirty old woman the next.

She'd told herself a hundred times it was just a sex thing. That it was just biology. She may have been a widow but she was still a woman. With needs.

For the love of Mike, she was thirty-four years old. Not a hundred and four.

Not dead.

Joss liked sex. She and Andy had always had an active sex life right up until a car had run a red light and taken him from her. And she'd been deprived of that for a long time. So surely it was only natural for that urge to return at some stage?

She *had* slept with a guy since Andy had died. On the first anniversary of his death, to be precise. That hadn't been about urges. She'd been drunk and sad and had needed a crutch.

But this. This…thing she felt when she looked at Troy was different. It was chemistry. Crazy and unfathomable but wholly undeniable. She remembered it well. Remembered the spark in her veins, the low drag in her belly, the tingle in her breasts.

Remembered how good it felt to have a man's weight pressing her into a mattress, a man's head between her legs, a man's hardness pounding inside her.

Remembered it as vividly as she remembered the trail of his finger on the back of her thigh.

She wasn't going to act on it. *She wasn't.* But it was there, nonetheless.

"Mom."

Joss groaned at Damien's not-so-quiet whisper right near her ear. She'd finally subsided into slumber sometime after the sun had started to pinken the sky, which felt like five minutes ago.

"Wake up, Mom." A brisk shake to her shoulder jiggled her eyelids open. Her son's spotty not-quite-a-boy-not-yet-a-man face filled her vision, the metal tracks on his teeth no longer foreign to either of them. "The guy from the other night is asleep on the couch."

Joss sighed. It hadn't been a bad dream. "Yes." She

stretched. "It's a long story."

Damien seemed to take that in his stride. "Pop said breakfast is almost ready."

"Okay." She rubbed her eyes and sat up, her bedside clock pronouncing it to be six-thirty. "Tell him I'm coming."

Joss swung her legs out of bed and grabbed for her short-sleeved cotton gown that came to just above her knees. Normally she wouldn't bother but with Troy in the house covering herself seemed like a sensible move.

Frying bacon greeted her as she padded down the hallway past the doorway into the living room. She refused to look his way but caught the bulk of his reclined body in her peripheral vision nevertheless. She entered the kitchen and Gus greeted her with a nod.

Her father-in-law was a strong, stocky man—considering his seventy years—with a dapper white goatee that always reminded her of Colonel Sanders. "Morning, Joss. We have a visitor I see."

"Yeah. Sorry 'bout that." She crossed to the ever-present coffee pot. She'd tried to introduce one of those modern pod machines but Gus was welded to his gut rot.

She relayed the story as she fixed her breakfast. Occasionally she joined Gus and Damien for heart attack on a plate but usually she stuck with yogurt and granola.

"He really is a bull rider?" Damien asked, a tremble of excitement in his voice.

Joss nodded. "He's the full cowboy."

"*Awesome.*"

"This the guy who brought the criminal mastermind home the other night?"

Damien had the good grace to blush. He'd copped an earful from his grandfather the next day and had spent the last two days working for Gus for free. Considering her father-in-law owned a fencing contractor business, Damien had been worked to the bone.

He still had the blisters.

"Yes."

Gus plonked down his plate loaded with bacon and two sunny-side up eggs. Damien was already halfway through his. Her son might have wanted to come to a rural backwater as much as he'd wanted to drill a hole in his head but he'd embraced his grandfather's breakfasts with gusto.

Which was probably just as well given how perennially hungry he was. Joss didn't seem to be able to fill him up these days.

"Good." Gus nodded his approval as he tucked into his food. "It's the least we could do for him."

Gus was just finishing up when Troy appeared in the doorway. He was bleary-eyed, rubbing his right hand over his hair, his biceps and abs shifting nicely. A flush of heat surged from the tips of her toes to the top of her head.

Sweet baby cheeses.

Maybe she was perimenopausal? Thirty-four was young but it wasn't unheard of…

He shot her a lazy smile. "Morning."

His low easy greeting reached out and touched her as surely as the finger that had stroked up the back of her thigh last night. She imagined how good it would be to hear that greeting every morning and gripped her mug tighter.

She hadn't realized how much she missed the intimacy of a relationship—not just the sex—until this second. Even something as simple as a good morning from a man not related to her popped the cork on a well of yearning.

"How did you sleep?" She kept her tone brisk and impersonal.

"Like a baby." He leaned his good shoulder into the frame. "You?"

She narrowed her eyes at him in warning. What was he doing flirting with her in front of Gus? "How's the elbow?"

He grimaced at his splinted arm. "Well I know it's there."

"You should take a couple more pills."

"Nah," he dismissed. "It's bearable."

Joss suppressed a snort. That was just stupid man code for hurts-like-hell-but-trying-to-look-brave. "I'll examine it before you go."

Which meant she was going to have to lay her hands on him. And hope like hell they didn't develop a mind of their own.

"Sure." He tipped his chin in Damien's direction. "Hey, mate."

Damien mumbled a greeting obviously still embarrassed by his history with Troy. Gus stood and ambled toward Troy. He reached his hand out as he neared. "I'm Gus."

Troy shook his hand. "Troy Jensen, sir."

Gus eyed him for a moment. "You got a shirt, son?"

"I do but…" He tapped the splint. "Think I need some coffee before I figure out the ins and outs of this thing."

Joss blinked as the older man honked out a laugh. Gus Garrity was small-town with a capital S. He *usually* held strangers in great suspicion. He certainly didn't take this easily to them. "Joss can help you with that later."

Joss would most definitely not help him with that later. Performing a cursory examination was going to be hard enough without becoming his damn nursemaid.

He was a big boy; he'd figure it out.

"You hungry?" Gus asked.

"Starving."

"You're not one of those fancy vegans are you?"

Joss suppressed a smile at the horrified expression on both men's faces. "No, sir."

Her father-in-law nodded briskly in approval. "Call me Gus." He pointed to the table. "Pull up a seat. I'll have it cooked in a jiffy."

He chose the one next to Joss—of course—which she refused to acknowledge. He was hard to ignore though with pheromones radiating off his body in waves. Thankfully Gus and Damien were full of questions about the rodeo and she didn't have to make conversation.

"What's your background, son?" Gus asked, placing another heaped plate of bacon and eggs on the table.

Joss wondered how Troy was going to manage to use utensils with his splinted arm. Normally she'd offer to help but, as with his shirt, she figured he'd work it out if he was hungry enough.

Evidently he was as he attacked the mound of food.

"That an Australian accent?"

"Yes, sir, it is."

"You learned to ride bulls back home?"

Troy nodded, his mouth full. Gus waited patiently while he swallowed. "I started working as a stockman on a big cattle property...that's like a ranch, when I was sixteen. I got into the rodeo circuit there before coming over to the States to try my luck seven years ago."

"Cattle property, huh?" Gus stroked his goatee, his gaze narrowing in on Troy. Joss knew that look. She wondered what the old coot was up to. "What are your plans now?"

"I was going to mosey on to Big Springs for the rodeo there next weekend but the doc here reckons I shouldn't compete for a few weeks. Hoping to make Lubbock in three weeks."

"Do you have a place you go to in breaks? Some kind of base? Family you go to?"

Troy paused to wash some food down with a cup of coffee Gus had put in front of him earlier. Joss still wasn't sure where this was going. "Not really." He shrugged as he speared more bacon. "Sometimes I head to one of the guys' ranches but otherwise I kinda just drift around in between rodeos. Head to the next town, check it out. A lot of the guys fly to events but I'm happy to drive. I like being out in the open."

He said it all very matter-of-fact and it certainly confirmed Joss's earlier opinion about him being a rolling stone. But it sounded so...lonely. America was a big country, a lot of big sky, open plains and deserted roads.

Her doctor bone tweaked and before she could stomp on it she said, "You don't have any family? Not even back home?"

His hesitation was almost imperceptible. Probably if she hadn't been sitting so close she might not have seen it at all. But she did.

"I usually head back to Oz for Christmas. Back to Forrester's Landing, that's the property I worked at. Aaron Forrester's my best mate and I usually crash with him although he's just gotten himself hitched so..."

He didn't finish the sentence but Joss did. *So he didn't want to be a third wheel?* That was sad. Even sadder was the way he'd deliberately avoided answering her question about his family.

"You're at a loose end, then?" Gus mused.

Troy nodded. "Apart from some physical therapy."

Gus drummed on the table. "I've got some good physical

therapy for you. Any good at fencing?"

Joss almost choked on her mouthful of coffee. She sat up straight in her chair and shook her head. "No, Gus."

Troy ignored her. "I can fence in my sleep."

"*Gus.*" She narrowed her eyes at her father-in-law who could be stubborn as a mule. "He dislocated his elbow. He shouldn't be doing any heavy lifting with his arm. Not to mention it's going to be in a splint for a couple of weeks."

"He's still got his right arm, don't he?"

"Yeah," Troy drawled, amusement flattening his vowels even more than usual. "I've still got my right arm."

She glared at Gus. "You want to take on a one-armed fencer?"

"Damien's got his summer job starting today so I'm losing my sidekick and Cody's out with his broken leg for another couple of weeks. It'd be handy to have even one extra hand on."

"I bet I can fence better one-armed than most men can with two."

There was no bravado to the claim. His expression was sincere and Joss believed him. She didn't doubt this man could do a crap ton of things better than most men.

"It's only temporary," Gus said. "Just some help with a couple of big jobs I have on. And I'll pay him."

"No, sir." Troy shook his head. "I've got more money than I know what to do with, I don't need yours as well. I'm just happy to help. Besides..." He flicked a sideways glance at Joss. "You know what they say about idle hands?"

Idle hands were the devil's tools.

It might have done him more credit had he actually looked like that was a bad thing. She tried really hard not to think about his hands and the kind of sinning she assumed they got up to on a regular basis.

If she'd ever met anyone more like the devil incarnate, Joss couldn't remember.

"Okay then. If you insist." Gus wasn't one to look a gift horse in the mouth. "But I must insist that you bunk with us."

"*What?*" Joss sat up abruptly. No way. *Sweet baby cheeses.* She'd boink him for sure.

"In the loft over the garage."

Joss gaped at her father-in-law. The loft? Was he insane? He barely knew Troy. There were people living in this town who'd been here for over a decade that Gus barely spoke to because they were *new folk* and now he was throwing his house open to some blow-in from *Australia?*

Ultimately though, this wasn't Joss's house and she didn't get to say who could stay.

Troy grinned, big and lazy, an intoxicating waft of cocky-young-guy enveloping her. "Thank you, Gus, I'd love to. I can pay rent though."

"Nonsense," Gus dismissed. "You work for free; you stay for free."

Joss shut her eyes briefly. *Awesome.* She was going to be

cohabiting with Troy Jensen. Of course, Gus would run him so ragged there'd be no time for his hands to become idle.

But what about hers?

Chapter Six

JOSS LEFT HALF an hour later to drop Damien into the Lunch Box, the town's newest diner. Normally he went everywhere round town on his bike but, as she'd confiscated it, she was his only form of transport. She should make him walk but getting out of the house right now was more important than principle.

Especially after those few minutes she'd spent examining Troy's arm. She'd kept it brief and impersonal, excruciatingly aware of Gus and Damien's interest in the proceedings. She doubted she'd ever been more stick-up-her-ass professional in all her days. But still she couldn't deny how much her insides had quaked as her fingers had fumbled with the splint strapping and then slid on to his skin.

Thankfully Joss had managed to convince both men during her examination that Troy should at least rest his arm for today and see the hospital physical therapist first about exercises before he took on any strenuous activity.

Troy had agreed but she could tell he was itching to get out with Gus. About as much as he was itching to get out of the splint, bitching about its bulk and inconvenience when she strapped it back in place, suggesting that he could go without during the day and just wear it at night.

"Two weeks," she'd intoned as she'd tightened the Velcro strapping. "Day and night. Rain, hail and shine. You can take it off for exercises and showering and that's it until I reassess in two weeks."

He hadn't been happy but Joss could live with that.

She was home again twenty minutes later to a blessedly silent house. Gus had volunteered to take Troy with him and drop him off at his vehicle on the way out to the Harris farm, which saved her any more contact with him. Troy was going to check out of the motel, pick up his stuff and make his way back to the house. She'd given him the PT number to ring and make an appointment.

Gus had left the kitchen spotless as always and she absently ran her hand over the flat wooden surface of the table. This house had been a sanctuary for her this past year and she'd been grateful to Gus—despite wanting to currently strangle him—for suggesting they make the move and start over.

Damien had been getting into more and more trouble in Chicago. He'd fallen in with the wrong crowd, was flunking grades and cutting class. He'd been given detention for being disruptive and disrespectful and had come home *drunk* from a couple of parties.

She'd been at her wits' end.

Having Gus's gruff, no-nonsense influence had helped a

little but Damien was still such a ball of anger. At her for forcing him to leave Chicago. At Gus for suggesting it. At Andy for dying.

Anger that would flare up and overwhelm him when she least expected it, fueled by a cocktail of raging hormones. It broke her heart seeing the little ten-year-old boy who'd just lost his father trapped inside. She could see him wanting to get out of the angry fifteen-year-old's body but he didn't know how.

She sighed, feeling impotent in the face of it but shook it off. She refused to be overwhelmed. They *would* get through this. In the meantime, she had work to do. The loft needed a spring-clean and she'd better do it before Troy got home.

The last thing she wanted was to be stuck up there with him. There wasn't much she could do about the unnatural fixation she'd developed on the guy but she could keep her exposure to him as limited as possible.

Five minutes later with an armful of linen, a bucket full of cleaning products and her earbuds pumping out Dixie Chicks, she climbed the steps to the loft. Gus had talked about letting Damien have the space in his senior year of high school and Joss had thought it a good idea but not unless he straightened out.

She wasn't about to reward delinquency with freedom.

With her burden obscuring her view, she groped for the handle and twisted the knob. The loft was never locked and the door gave easily. She didn't notice the boots at the front door as she hummed along to the music, crossing straight to the bed to dump her armload on the bare mattress.

She didn't notice the partially fogged vanity mirror as she walked toward the bathroom, either—two thick fluffy towels in hand. Not until she was inside anyway and a pair of jeans and fringed leather chaps tossed carelessly over the edge of the vanity came into view.

She almost dropped the towels as she spun around.

"Hey."

The Dixie Chicks crooning, *there's your trouble,* straight into her ear was a particularly ironic twist.

Joss yanked the earbuds out as she gaped at the man standing in the open doorway of the shower cubicle. Thankfully he was wearing a towel—even if it was positioned sinfully low on his hips.

But that still left an awful lot to look at. An *awful* lot. Like the scattered droplets of water on his shoulders and chest and abs. And his nipples. Flat and brown and so evenly spaced she wanted to get out a ruler and measure them.

Or possibly use her tongue.

He cocked an eyebrow, the tiny white scar stupid sexy in the daylight. "Finished?"

"I…I…"

She swallowed but it was no good, the ability to talk seemed to have deserted her. He took a step toward her and Joss took a hasty step back, bringing her right up against the vanity. Her heart beat a frantic tattoo in her chest.

Sweet baby cheeses. He was big and it was a very, very small bathroom.

The aroma of soap and shampoo had replaced leather and rope and her stomach clenched. She'd always been a sucker for that man-just-out-of-the-shower smell. She clutched the towels to her chest as if they might protect her from it.

"I thought you'd gone with Gus?"

"He had to leave in a hurry and I really needed a shower." He took another step toward her. One more and they'd be hip to hip. "I was really dirty."

The way he was crowding her back, his provocative choice of words should be horrifying and intimidating. She should be mad as hell, demanding he stop. Demanding he take a step back. But with his long, lean body looming, *her* body was melting down.

She didn't want him to stop or step back. She wanted him to come closer. To press his body along hers. To feel all his heat and hardness right up in her face.

And parts much lower.

She shouldn't want it. It was…pure madness. But she did. Her hands trembled with the effort *not* to touch him.

"If I'd known you'd be along," he said, his voice low and lazy, "I would have waited for assistance. It's not easy showering one-handed."

A slew of images all involving him wet and naked and soapy and the things he *could* do one-handed, cluttered up her brainpower. "And yet you managed." Her voice was nothing more than a raspy whisper.

"Sure. I'm a self-sufficient kinda guy. But..." He took the last step, an inch of air separating his thighs from hers. "It's much more fun with two."

Joss's heart was pounding so furiously she was sure he must be able to feel the vibrations hitting him in the chest. "I just came to give the loft a bit of a spring-clean. Bring some sheets and towels."

She clung to the last bit of sanity she had and hoped like hell he'd do the right thing and back the hell up.

He didn't.

Instead he spread his arms out—his injured elbow hampering the movement on the left. "I found one. As you can see."

Which automatically dragged her gaze down.

Down. Down. Down.

Over his neck and his chest and his abs. Oh yes he had. And didn't he wear the hell out of it.

He reached for the towels she was using as a shield and prized them gently from her grasp, shoving them on top of his jeans and chaps.

"You smell *great*," he murmured, his good hand sliding onto the vanity near her hip, his injured arm bent and skewed awkwardly out as his lips dropped to the side of her neck.

She smelled great? This from the man who smelled like a

deodorant commercial.

Joss shut her eyes as his lips buzzed her skin. For a ridiculously light touch she felt it *everywhere*. In her breasts and thighs and deep behind her belly button.

"Like candy canes."

Part of Joss recognized it was probably just her mouthwash he could smell but the other part—the part that was already tipping her head to the side to give him better access—was thinking maybe she should start bathing in the stuff.

His hand left the vanity and crept up her side and around to her back as his thighs pressed against hers, lean and hard. His fingertips grabbed the end of her ponytail and gently tugged, angling her head back even further.

"I love candy canes," he muttered, his breath warm as his tongue stroked the sensitive skin at the angle of her jaw. "I love sucking on them." His lips closed over her earlobe and tugged.

A sound came from the back of her throat. Something quite unholy—half wanton, half feral. It joined the jungle beat in her head and the rising urge to submit. Joss was powerless to do anything other than turn her face and seek the heat and oblivion of his mouth.

"*Troy.*"

"What, Joss?" His hand grabbed more of her ponytail, elongating her throat, his mouth taking full advantage as his body settled against hers, the hard jut of his erection pushing urgently against her belly. "What do you want?" he whispered against the thick thud of her carotid pulse. "Tell me what you want, baby."

No one had ever called her baby. The fact that it had come from a guy seven years her junior should have been ridiculous. But it wasn't. *It curled her toes.*

"Kiss me."

Before even the next beat of her heart, his mouth was on hers. Not slow and sweet but fast and urgent. Joss moaned, her body flooding with the wild sexual thrill of it, her hands circling his waist to pull him closer.

Oh yes. *She remembered this.* The soft and the hard of a man's mouth, the frenzy of tangling tongues, the pulse-fluttering excitement of a big, firm body unapologetically violating personal space.

The kiss deepened. Joss slid her hands to Troy's butt, stroking him through the towel. His glutes tightened. Her nipples hardened. His hand fell to her upper thigh, slipping behind to where leg met ass. He squeezed and lifted, opening up her hips, stepping boldly into the gap, notching himself between her thighs, his hand urging her up onto the vanity before sliding to the base of her spine.

He held her there *tight* as he ground his erection into her, a bolt of pure pleasure striking her core. Joss moaned, tightening her thighs around his hips, locking her ankles around his ass, silently demanding more.

He gave it, grinding slow and deliberate against her center as his tongue slid down her windpipe. She shivered as his lips made their way to the spot just below her ear. "You've made me so hard, Joss," he whispered.

She whimpered deep in her throat at the dizzying compliment. She wanted to see that. Feel it. Even the thought of it tripped a switch inside, her lips seeking his in reckless abandon. He took them, groaning into her mouth, his head twisting, his lips hunting, owning her and the kiss within seconds.

If anyone had told Joss last week that she'd be dry humping a twenty-seven-year-old she'd met only five days prior in the bathroom of the loft above her garage, she'd have committed them for psychiatric evaluation. But here she was and she *could not* get enough.

Her body *throbbed* with need. Maybe *she* needed committing?

But not before she'd kissed him a little longer, explored him a little further. It'd been so long since she'd been with a man, her whole body trembled with the need to touch him.

Touch all of him.

Of their own volition, her hands pushed between their bodies just above where his crotch was grinding maddeningly slow against hers. Her fingers found the knot of the towel, loosened it, pulled it open, revealing the hot hard length of him.

He gasped, breaking off the kiss as she wrapped her fingers around him. "*Jeeeeesus,*" he muttered, his lips at her neck, his breath ragged.

Joss's eyes practically rolled back in her head at the catch in his voice and the way he filled her palm.

This.

This is what she wanted. What she needed. *What she'd missed.*

The feel of an aroused man thick and hard in her hand. Knowing she was responsible. Knowing she could bring him to his knees.

She'd forgotten how heady it was.

She glanced down between them, satisfied to see his plump head flushed with arousal and leaking fluid. It was as long and lean and hard as the rest of him and she squeezed, smearing the bead of liquid with her thumb.

"*Joss.*"

His voice caught, warm and husky on her neck, full of need. And damned if she didn't want to hear him say it again. Just like that—low and throaty. She squeezed him again, taking her time to ease her loaded fist from root to tip.

He groaned her name this time. "*Jossss.*"

Another spurt of pleasure—of power—intoxicated her senses and she stroked him all the way down and all the way up again.

His jerky breath hit her system like a drug and she was in thrall. Of his potency. And hers. She didn't want to stop. She wanted to keep going, keep touching him like this until he lost control. She wanted to bring him to his knees, this cocky young guy who called her baby and made her want things she hadn't even realized she'd been missing.

Her heart hammered like a piston as she slid her hand up and down one more time, watching the movement, utterly transfixed by the intimacy of the act, by the petal softness of skin stretched taut over a steely girth. Her breath sawed in and out, hot and heavy in lungs that felt too big for her chest.

"You're driving me crazy." His ragged words were barely louder than a whisper but wicked hot against her neck.

And he didn't sound cocky or so sure of himself now. He sounded completely at her mercy.

Like he might just die if she stopped.

He lifted his head, their gazes locking, the heated jade of his eyes revealing an agony of pleasure. His eyes fluttered closed for a second or two as she set a determined rhythm with her hand.

"I feel I have to warn you," he murmured, his eyelids opening as if they weighed a ton. "If you keep that up it's going to get real messy."

Joss's pulse leapt. *Yes.* She picked up the pace, drawing a grunt from the back of his throat. He reached for the hem of her T-shirt, peeling it up. "You have too many clothes on."

"No."

Joss shook her head. This whole thing was crazy. No need to make it crazier by involving her any more than she was. She could do this. Have this moment and walk away.

But only if it was about him.

"Just this."

"Just what?" His voice rumbled around her, his mouth brushing her neck and her chin and her mouth.

"This," she muttered, sliding faster, squeezing harder. "I want to…watch you."

It had been a long time since she'd held a man's sexual pleasure in the palm of her hand. God…it had been a very long time since she'd been anything other than a mother or a doctor or a goddamned widow.

Since a man had looked at her with such frank desire.

He groaned in her ear as she worked him faster, his good hand planted firmly in the middle of her back. "Then do it." His voice was like sandpaper against her skin. "But don't stop, baby. Don't you *dare* stop until I'm done."

Joss whimpered at the bald demand, wetness flooding between her legs, a roar of feminine power flooding her veins.

She wouldn't stop. She wouldn't stop until he begged her to.

She gripped him harder. *Faster.*

"*Fuuuck*, baby," he whispered, his lips pressed to her throat.

His casual use of the *f* word was like a dose of accelerant to the inferno in her veins. It shouldn't be. People in these parts believed you went to hell for cussing.

God alone knew where she'd end up after giving a hand

job to a virtual stranger.

"Oh…God…*yesss.*" The words puffed against her skin, hot and desperate.

His hips rocked. Her pulse hammered. He thrust into her hand. Her lungs burned.

"*Christ.*" He panted into her neck, his glutes trembling beneath the firm hold of her calves. She stroked and stroked as he thrust and thrust. "*Yesss,*" he hissed, throwing his head back as his entire body trembled. "Fuck. Yes. *Fuck.* I'm coming."

Joss almost came just from the dirty words he was using as a jet of warm ejaculate splattered his belly. "Jesus…*baby.*" He groaned deep and low. "I'm coming."

"Yes." A burst of feminine power, fierce and triumphant, ripped through her chest as a second stream spurted from his cock.

She'd done this to him. *She'd* made him come. She'd made him cuss and blaspheme and call out to Jesus.

She plowed her free hand into the back of his hair, gripping him tight at the nape, anchoring his forehead in the crook of her neck, as she finished him off. Stroking and stroking until there was nothing left.

Until he wrenched her hand away and begged her to stop.

Chapter Seven

TROY'S PULSE THUNDERED through his ears, his breathing like a tornado in the small bathroom as all the scattered parts of his anatomy slowly came back together again.

Although he doubted they'd ever go back the same way.

That had been intense. *She'd* been intense. Hell, he'd had full-on sex that hadn't been that intense.

It had been fucking *tantric*.

If Joss could do *that* with just a hand job then he was sunk for sure. "You are a goddess." His mouth brushed the point where her neck met her shoulder and a shiver trembled through her body. Gooseflesh puckered her skin, tickling his lips.

She huffed out a husky half laugh, her ankles unlocking from behind him. "I guess I'm not as rusty as I thought."

Troy eased himself back. She met his eyes shyly, her gray gaze wary. "I think there are some things you just don't forget."

"Like how messy a hand job can be."

She glanced down and he followed suit. His flesh prickled in awareness as her eyes skimmed his chest and abs, streaked with the evidence of his orgasm.

"Sorry."

Troy blinked. *Sorry? He* wasn't. That had been the goddamn gold standard of hand jobs and if a bull killed him tomorrow, he'd die a happy man.

She reached over to the towels he'd taken off her earlier and passed him one, using one end to wipe her hand as he fixed himself up, his hips still firmly wedged between her thighs. He re-tied the towel at his waist, sucking in a swift breath as his elbow twinged.

"God. Your elbow..." Her cheeks pinked up. "I hope I didn't... Is it okay?"

Troy had been so blissed out he doubted he'd have felt it being amputated. He sure as hell didn't want to talk about it now. Not standing between Joss's thighs and two hours until his physical therapy appointment.

"Trust me, I was feeling no pain." His good hand found her ponytail again, winding it around his palm. "Now..." He pulled gently and her neck stretched out nicely for his pleasure. "Where were we?"

"Oh no." She resisted the tug and shoved against his chest. "Let me up."

"What's your rush?" He lowered his head and nuzzled down the slender ridge of her throat. "I'm just getting started."

Troy was gratified to feel the bob of her throat beneath

his lips. "I'm...good."

He chuckled against the soft spot where throat met jaw. "I'm thinking giving me a hand job in your bathroom makes you bad. Very, very bad."

"Troy." She pushed on his shoulders and Troy reluctantly pulled his lips from her neck. "Look. We got carried away. That's understandable. You were practically naked and this is a very small bathroom. We have...chemistry."

Troy laughed at her understatement. "I've been wanting to kiss you ever since I saw you with that lug wrench. I could tell even then you were good with your hands."

She shot him a prim look down her nose, clearly not going to get down in the mud with him. "I'm a thirty-four-year-old widow with a fifteen-year-old kid. You're a twenty-seven-year-old bull rider—"

"So?"

Her cheeks heated. "I just gave you—someone I didn't even know five days ago—a hand job in my father-in-law's house."

He grinned at her. "I won't tell anyone if you don't."

"I don't do this kind of thing." She glared at him obviously exasperated. "I have a job and a community and roots. You drift through life with no family, no *roots,* no home. I don't do casual sex. That's *all* you do. At the moment all we have in common is an appreciation for lug wrenches and hand jobs. There's nothing compatible about us, Troy."

"Oh yeah? You don't think I don't know how wet you

are right now?"

She dropped her gaze. "That's just sex." She waved it away with her hand like sexual compatibility wasn't an important consideration.

Like it wasn't something rare and unique. Troy had indulged himself a lot since he'd lost his virginity at fourteen. He'd had all kinds of sex in all kinds of ways and most of it had been empty and only momentarily satisfying.

He could still feel the hum in his cells from the orgasm she'd yanked out of him. And the strange jungle beat of his heart.

"So you're telling me your body's not screaming for fulfillment now? That if I slid my hands between your legs that I couldn't get you off in ten seconds flat? That you're not going to touch yourself tonight as you lie in bed thinking about how hard you made me come?"

She shut her eyes for a moment and Troy didn't have to be inside her head to know his words had affected her. Hell…he'd given *himself* a hard-on.

Her knuckles had whitened suddenly and he could see her nipples, two hard little dots, straining against the fabric of her T-shirt.

Her eyes flicked open, gray gaze steely and determined. "Let me up." He sighed and took two steps back and one to the side, his arms semi-raised in surrender.

She slid off the vanity, her ponytail bobbing. "Look…we just had this *perfect* moment. This perfect *memory*. It was hot and fast and dirty and I wouldn't change a damn thing."

Troy nodded in total agreement. He wouldn't either.

"I'm going to bring that thing out next time Damien tells me hates me or after I've had to tell some parents that their kid is paralyzed from a car crash and it's going to put a smile on my face again. I don't want to ruin its flawlessness with the train wreck that will come after if I let this become sex or a fling or anything other than one perfect moment."

Troy regarded her silently. What she said made a lot of sense. Their reality had gotten lost in the heady sexuality of the moment. He was moving on and she was firmly rooted here.

With her kid.

For a crazy ten minutes he'd forgotten she was anything other than a desirable woman. And she was right. There were so few perfect moments in life—maybe being the star of someone else's was enough.

Given her look of grim determination, it would have to be.

"Fine." He sighed. She was right. He knew she was right. "But you pick up a lug wrench again in my company and all bets are off."

JOSS HEARD GUS'S truck pull up outside at five on the dot. Two car doors *thunked* shut seconds later and she mentally prepared herself for the impact of a tired, sweaty Troy wearing the hell out of a pair of jeans. Between that and the images in her head of him in nothing but a towel, it had been more trying having him around than she'd ever imagined.

And he'd only been with them four nights.

It didn't help that she wasn't used to having a man around the house anymore. Not the fit, virile variety anyway. His boots at the door, a waft of leather and rope when she least expected it, his sexy Calvin Kleins hanging on the line next to Gus's large striped boxer shorts all combined to keep her on edge.

There seemed to be a piece of him around every corner and Joss wondered how long it would take to erase him when he left. The physical signs of him anyway. She knew she'd never be able to erase him from her head—he was indelibly etched into her memory banks and she would always hold that moment in the bathroom close to her heart.

"It's good to be home, love," Gus said as he opened the back door and spotted her shelling peas from the garden at the table.

He said the same thing every day without fail and generally she agreed with the sentiment. But it felt like her home wasn't her own anymore as was quickly proven by the appearance of Troy, his splinted arm in no way detracting from the coiled energy of him.

Gus turned and whacked Troy in the stomach. "You

should ask Joss if she wants to go."

Joss startled. This *did not* sound good. "Ask me if I want to go where?"

"Johnny Duggan was out at the Harris farm today and he recognized Troy. Asked him to be his special guest at the steakhouse tonight."

John Duggan was the owner of the finest eating establishment in town—the Bull Bar.

"You know, sign a few autographs, shoot the breeze with the customers, that kind of thing."

"That's nice," Joss said noncommittally, keeping her gaze fixed on the peas. "I'm sure Troy doesn't need me holding his hand. He's a big boy."

As soon as the words were out she could have bitten her tongue off. She didn't dare look at Troy. She didn't have to. She could feel his gaze on her face, sense his laughter bubbling just below his surface.

She knew from intimate experience just how big that boy was.

"Oh…" Gus shifted from foot to foot, his mouth moving a couple of times as if he wanted to say something but didn't know how. "Well, sure…but Damien's not home from work until ten and it's Thursday, night. Half price grills."

Joss glanced up from her peas, narrowing her eyes at her father-in-law. He was acting strangely, pussyfooting around something. Gus didn't do pussyfooting. He was wincingly direct.

"You have company don't you?"

He shrugged nonchalantly. Gus didn't do nonchalant either. "Linda did say as she might drop in."

Ah. Now it made sense. Gus had been widowed a very long time—Andy's mother had died when Andy was six and Gus had been true to her all this time. Since Joss had arrived on the scene she'd encouraged him to get out more. It had been obvious that her father-in-law was lonely and while her and Damien had filled that hole to a degree there were different types of lonely.

She knew that well enough.

Gus's face was a little weathered from the sun but he still looked reasonably youthful for his age, was as fit as a fiddle and loved to line dance. Linda Wells was his age, had been widowed for eight years, made the best sweet tea in town and also loved to line dance.

More importantly, they liked each other. Which made them pretty damn perfect couple material. They'd just needed a gentle nudge. Which is what she'd been doing. Although the pace had still been slower than a wet week so Joss sure as hell didn't want to cramp their style tonight.

"What time did she say she might be dropping by?"

"I believe she mentioned seven."

Joss suppressed a smile at Gus's casual affect. He wasn't fooling her for a moment. "All right then." She eyed Troy. The last thing she wanted to do was go out with him in a social situation but Troy would be gone soon and Gus and Linda would still be here. She could while away a few hours in his company without wanting to do him.

Probably.

"Shall we leave about quarter to seven?"

That wide grin did not bode well. It emphasized his crooked nose and gave him a devilish air. But he nodded all nice and polite in front of a distracted Gus. "Yes, ma'am."

JOHN DUGGAN PUMPED Troy's hand when they arrived just before seven. He was a big man with a salt and pepper handlebar moustache and he was wearing his regulation ten-gallon hat. "Do you mind if I whisk this man away from you for a few minutes, Doc Garrity? There are some people who are dying to meet him."

Troy looked like he was about to object but she beat him to the punch. "Not at all, John." She smiled at him genially. "Send me over a glass of wine and you can take all the time you want."

John laughed in his big guffawing way. "I'll get the girls to bring it right on over and don't you worry, I'll have him back lickety-split."

It was fifteen minutes before John made good on his word. Joss didn't mind. The booth seats were comfortable, Lady Antebellum played through hidden speakers and the longer Troy was away the less she had to look at him. He was wearing his best dress jeans and a blue and green paisley button-down shirt that accentuated his eyes and fit his lean chest to perfection. His hat—apparently called an Akubra—was pulled low on his forehead.

John chatted for a few more minutes and took their orders before he departed. "You never told me they had a mechanical bull." Troy sipped a beer he'd brought to the table.

Joss frowned. "I didn't know they had. It must be new."

He grinned at her suggestively and she shook her head. "Oh no you don't, buster—absolutely no riding bulls of any variety. Your PT would have a fit."

"I wasn't talking about me."

"Oh hell no." She shook her head again, even more vehemently. "I'm wearing a skirt in case you hadn't noticed." The last thing she wanted was to flash her ass to half the town as she was tossed off.

His gaze dropped to where the foot of her crossed leg stuck out from the edge of the booth, the fringe of her peasant-style skirt fanned over her ankle. "Oh I noticed."

His voice dropped an octave and Joss's insides melted like marshmallow being slowly roasted over a campfire.

"Besides, I don't know a bull's head from its ass and I'm not getting on one, mechanical or otherwise."

He tsked. "Such a city girl."

She refused to let his teasing go to her head. "Chicago

born and bred."

"It must have been a shock to come to a place with less than twenty thousand people."

"Yes and no. We'd visited on and off over the years so I knew the town but a permanent move was still a big deal. I don't think Damien's forgiven me yet and it's been a year."

"He misses his mates?"

"Yeah well...I don't miss his *mates*." Joss's lips twisted at the thought of the company Damien had started to keep. "They were trouble and I didn't want him heading into the gutter, or *worse* with them."

"That why you moved?"

"Yes. Plus Gus was lonely; I could hear it in his voice. What about you? You country down to your bootstraps?"

"No. I was born and bred in Sydney, actually. Didn't go out to the Top End until I was sixteen. I didn't know the ass end of a bull either."

Joss blinked. "So you went from city boy to rookie champion on the national circuit here in the States in four years?"

He cocked an eyebrow and Joss's gaze was once again drawn to the white scar that slashed it in half. "You been Googling me?"

Joss's cheeks warmed. "I needed to know I wasn't letting an axe murderer into our house."

He snorted. "Yes," he said, getting the conversation back on track. "I took to bull riding like a duck to water."

"I would have thought to be that good it'd have to be in your blood."

"A lot of guys do start at a really early age. But—" He shrugged. "It isn't all about practice. It's about nerve and steel and a complete disregard for your own safety."

She leaned forward, her elbow on the table, her chin propped on her palm. "And that's you, isn't it?"

Even at this short acquaintance she could see it. He may have perfected the art of laid-back but his reckless streak bubbled not that far below his surface.

"I've been known to get in the odd scrape or two."

"How did a kid from the city end up on a massive cattle station? You wanted to be a cowboy?"

He snorted. "Ah no. It was the *last* thing I wanted to do."

"Oh?"

"Yes. Oh."

"You're not going to elaborate?"

He stared at her for long moments as if he was weighing her up, his gaze dark and brooding before he sighed and gathered himself. "I was more or less forced to go."

Joss frowned, a prickle at the base of her spine. "Forced?"

"It was kind of my last chance before I ended up in juvie."

Joss sat back in her seat at the admission. "Juvie?" Now that she hadn't expected.

He nodded. "I was quite the delinquent."

Images from the night she'd pulled open the front door to find Troy standing on the other side came back to her. He'd been standing tall on her doorstep, confident and patient. Not angry or vengeful, not judgmental of her or Damien. But not apologetic either.

Like a man who had been there before and understood the psyche of a teenage boy, understood the need for discipline and consequences.

Interesting.

It was hard not to see parallels between Troy and Damien. Maybe having Troy around would be good for her son. A living example of how things could work out if you gave them a chance.

"Did you…" Joss didn't know what she should ask or even if she had a right to. And frankly she wasn't sure she wanted to know the answers. "What did you…?"

"What did I do?" He shrugged. "What didn't I do? I lied, I conned, I got into fights. I stole. All kinds of things. Bags and money and jewelry and even cars from time to time. I spent most of my teenage years either drunk or stoned. I rarely went to school, I was in and out of the system and I was buying drugs for my parents by the time I was eight."

He said it so casually, as if the words meant nothing to him, as if he was immune to them. But his face was a mask and behind it, she suspected, there was a world of pain.

If he'd ripped her heart out of her chest, Joss couldn't have felt any more wretched for him.

Silence settled in the space between them. Troy had told her he didn't have any family and she could see why. Even if his parents were still around, why would he want anything to do with people who'd exposed him to that kind of life?

Delinquents were made, not born.

She knew the answers of course. She'd grown up in Chicago. Worked in the hospitals there. But it didn't make it any less heart wrenching.

"I'm sorry," she said eventually. It was hopelessly inadequate but it came from the bottom of her heart.

He lifted a shoulder in a dismissive gesture. "You don't have to worry. I'm not that guy anymore."

"I'm not worried."

She'd met some scary dudes in inner-city hospitals. Edgy guys with chips on their shoulders bristling with anger and anarchy. Guys who put a real itch up her spine. But there was nothing remotely edgy about Troy.

Whoever he'd been for sixteen years was plainly not who he was now. He'd proved that over and over. Stopping to help her with her tire. Bringing Damien home that night. Working for Gus for free.

Even letting her call the shots in the bathroom without getting pushy and pissed off.

No. She wasn't worried about the kind of man Troy Jensen was. She was too busy worrying about the leap in her pulse whenever he was around.

Chapter Eight

"SO...YOU ENDED UP on a ranch?" Joss prompted.

"Yes." He took a mouthful of beer. "My case worker knew this guy, Martin Forrester, and convinced him to take me on for a couple of months at his cattle property."

"You didn't like it?"

"Hell no. That first month I was a right pain in the ass. But Martin's a tough old guy. Big on discipline and personal responsibility. He didn't take any of my shit and the more I kicked up, the harder he drove me. Then one day he was so pissed off with something I'd done, he pointed to the meanest bull I'd ever seen in my life and said, "All right, dickhead. Let's see how shit hot you really are."

He smiled at the memory and it was so warm and genuine Joss couldn't help but smile back. "What happened then?"

"He dared me to ride it for eight seconds."

"And did you?"

"Hell no. It tossed me in two seconds. But it was the most exhilarating two seconds of my life and I was hooked. And he had me because I'd do just about anything to get on the back of a bull and he used it shamelessly to bend me to his will. Turned me into a half decent cowboy pretty quickly after that."

He laughed and shook his head as he pressed the bottle to his mouth again. Joss wondered how those cool lips would feel pressed between her thighs and squirmed in her seat.

"Sounds like he knew what he was doing."

"Oh yeah, he's a canny old bastard."

She smiled at the obvious affection. "He means a lot to you."

He nodded, his gaze serious. "There isn't anything I wouldn't do for Martin Forrester. For the whole Forrester family. They saved my life."

The depth of his sincerity and insight held her in his thrall, their eyes locked. Who'd have thought stark honesty could be such a freaking turn-on? She wanted to stand up, grab his shirt and haul him and his mouth across the booth.

But their dinner arrived at that precise moment, saving them both from a public display of affection she probably wouldn't live down in this town all the years of her life. She either knew or was vaguely acquainted with seventy-five percent of the people in the room and the town thrived on gossip.

She quizzed him about the ranch as they ate and he kept her entertained with hair-raising stories of what he and Aaron Forrester had gotten up to in the *Top End,* as he called it, including a spot of croc wrestling.

No wonder he rode bulls for a living.

If even half of those stories were true, Troy was obviously a total adrenaline junkie.

She wondered if crime had given him the same kind of buzz and that's why he rode bulls—finding another way to get that high. She supposed there was a certain type of woman who was in to that kind of stuff and it was entertaining as heck to listen to. But a lot harder to be the other half, she imagined.

Was that why he was still single? Or was he just having too much fun to settle with one woman?

"Earth to Joss?"

Joss blinked. She'd drifted into her head and hadn't heard Troy. "Sorry, what were you saying?"

He laughed. "I think I've been saying too much. Tell me about you."

"There's nothing much exciting in my life, I'm afraid. It's all pretty boring. No crocodile wrestling in my past."

"No but you must have had Damien when you were eighteen or nineteen, yes? And still you became a doctor? That's not nothing."

"*Oh.*" She nodded her head in faux seriousness. "You want to hear about the exciting struggles of a teenage mother?"

He laughed again. "I admire you, is all. That can't have been an easy juggle?"

Joss's belly flipped at the compliment. This guy had a

unique ability to turn her on with the most un-sexy words on the planet. "It did throw a bit of a spanner in the works. I was nineteen. Andy and I had only been going out for a couple of months. I met him on campus. He was studying architecture."

She smiled remembering how proud Andy had been to be the only one in his family to have gone to college. "For two supposedly smart people we were pretty dumb."

"Sex makes people dumb."

Joss laughed. Never had truer words been spoken. "That's deep there, cowboy."

"Hey." He grinned. "I have layers, you know."

Oh yeah, he was a regular onion.

"Anyway…we were in love and the baby was ours and we wanted him from those first pink stripes on the preg test so we just made it work. We got married, kept studying. I dropped down to part time. It took me almost nine years and we were drowning in a huge mortgage and student loans and we couldn't have been happier."

He smiled. "It's sounds nice."

Her chest ached with nostalgia and squeezed at the streak of wistfulness in his voice. Her life had been a clambake by comparison. "It was."

"Do you mind me asking how he died?"

Joss shook her head. "No, I don't mind. It was a car accident. It was winter in Chicago—the roads were icy. He was waiting at a red light, the car behind him lost control and plowed into Andy, pushing him across the intersection just as a car was coming through."

As long as Joss lived she'd never forget opening the door to those two stony-faced police officers.

"I'm sorry. That must have been very difficult for you both."

After reassuring him she was fine to talk about it, Joss felt absurdly like crying. Not from the startling depth of his empathy but because he'd been sensitive to the fact that it hadn't just been her loss.

"It was."

"And you moved here a year ago. Because of Damien?"

Joss nodded. "If you'd asked me a few months prior to our move if I'd ever leave Chicago I would have told you no. *Hell* no. But I was just holding it all together there. I was able to pay down some of our debt from Andy's life insurance but there was still a lot owing, which made money even tighter without a second income."

Even now the financial stress of that time was enough to make her shudder.

"So I increased my shifts at the hospital, which was a real juggle with Damien's needs. And then he went and got himself possessed by some horrible demonic teen spirit and I'm pretty sure exorcisms are illegal so when Gus suggested we move to Plainview it was the next best thing."

His warm chuckle soothed the memory of frazzled nerves. "If you're after the opinion of a single, male bull rider who has no intention of ever having any rug rats, which—" He waggled his eyebrows. "—I'm sure you are. He's a good kid, Joss."

She gave him her best cut-the-crap look. "You caught him trying to steal money from your car."

"Yeah, but he was really bad at it. Which tells me he hadn't been doing a lot of it. And, by the way he was absolutely shitting himself on the way to your place. He was terrified of you finding out."

"Great. So my kid's scared of me?"

"That's a good thing," he assured hastily. "It means he knows there are going to be consequences. Nothing much scared me." He stared at his beer bottle, his thumb rubbing absently along the label. "Not repercussions or what people thought. I really just...didn't care what happened to me. Damien *cared*. He cared a lot."

Joss was both saddened for teen Troy and immeasurably bolstered by adult Troy's assurances.

From his lips to God's ears.

"He's angry." She sighed. "About his father dying. But then I suppose so were you."

"I wasn't angry. I was numb."

It was a chilling admission and Joss shivered at how empty it sounded. And what a contrast it was to the warm, funny, laid-back guy she'd come to know.

"Was he always?"

Joss frowned, struggling to follow his question, caught

up for a moment in the desolation of Troy's terrible past.

"Angry," he prompted. "About his father's death?"

"Oh. No." She fiddled with the stem of her wineglass. "He was sad…distraught actually, when it first happened. He was only ten. But then he took on this protective role of me. I think Gus must have told him he was the man of the house now or something."

He'd been so sweet back then, always checking on her, always worried about her feeling sad. He used to make her cards every day at school to cheer her up.

"But I guess all sweet ten-year-old boys eventually grow into pubescent teens, and money was tight so I was working a lot and he resented that and therefore me by association. And I think he really missed not having a man to talk to about guy stuff so he felt Andy's loss all over again, not as a boy but as a young man trying to find his way. He has Gus now but it's not the same."

"Sure." Troy nodded. "But most importantly, he has you."

"Yeah…" She shook her head. "I'm not sure he sees it that way."

"Trust me, he will. You and your love and your approval and support and even your discipline will get him through this. Damien's on the top of a slippery slope but the difference between him and me is that I didn't have a mother who loved me. Who was on my side. So don't underestimate yourself, okay?"

Joss was extraordinarily touched by Troy's words. Touched and saddened for little boy Troy who'd been dealt such a shitty hand. "Well thank you." She smiled hoping like crazy her eyes weren't bright and glassy. "But do you think we can talk about something else? This is supposed to be an enjoyable night out, right?"

He smiled. "Of course. *I'd* like to hear some funny medical stories. You must have some of them?"

"Plenty. Including a pineapple in a place a pineapple should never go."

"Jesus." His eyes bugged and she suppressed laughter. "How the fuck did a pineapple get up there?"

"Slipped in the shower."

He thought about it for a moment then frowned. "*What?*"

Joss laughed. "They always slip in the shower."

He laughed too and they spent the next half an hour discussing some of Joss's more risqué medical stories.

"So tell me, what's it like?" Joss asked as their plates were being cleared. "Being on a wild bucking bull? What's it *really* like?"

He sat back in the booth and studied her for a beat or two. "When I was a kid, me and my delinquent mates used to play chicken with the cars on the major highway near where we used to live. We'd choose peak hour and bolt across it, full pelt. It was a high-octane rush. I'd be absolutely shitting myself on the way across but it was totally exhilarating when I got to the other side. I felt like Superman. Which is exactly how it feels to ride a pissed-off bull."

Joss gaped at him. It was miracle Troy Jensen had survived his childhood. "As an ER doctor I have to tell you that sounds completely terrifying. You could have been killed."

He grinned. "But I wasn't."

She realized then that what she'd thought was a reckless streak was more like a death wish.

"You want to know what it's like?" He tipped his chin in the direction of the mechanical bull. "Hop on that thing. It'll give you some idea."

Joss glanced over to the cushioned ring that had been set up around the stylized metallic bull's torso. "Hell no."

He shot her an indolent look as he tucked his fist under the armpit of his good arm and flapped it like a wing. "*Bok. Bok, bok, bok.*"

"Seriously?" She folded her arms. "How old are you?"

Oh yeah…twenty-seven. *Sweet baby cheeses.*

"C'mon, Joss…" His hand crept across the table toward her. "You know you want to."

"I seriously don't. Plus I'm really uncoordinated."

His hand slid onto her folded arm and every nerve ending in the proximity went into rapture. "*J-ossssss.*" He sung it lightly, teasing her.

"Do I look stupid to you? That thing is just plain crazy."

"And when was the last time you did something crazy?"

Joss cocked an eyebrow. Was he kidding? "You have to

ask?"

A slow lazy grin warmed his face. "That wasn't crazy. That was hot."

She rolled her eyes. He *would* say that, wouldn't he? "My skirt."

"Is long." He dismissed it with a wave of his hand. "Too long to flash anything when you fall off."

"*When* huh?"

He nodded. "When."

"I'm more worried it might end up above my head."

He laughed but stopped abruptly when she glared at him. "I promise I won't look when you get tossed."

Joss glanced around her at the full restaurant. "And what about the other hundred people in here?"

"Oh come on." He affected an air of fake severity. "Good decent southern folk would surely avert their eyes from a lady in a state of undress."

She snorted. Half the men in here would trample over their wives for a glimpse of panties.

"Come on." He stood and held out his hand. "Let me show you why I do it."

And in that moment she wanted to know. To understand why a guy would risk death every night for some kind of cheap thrill. "Fine." She stood, ignoring his hand. "But if I break something I'm suing you."

He laughed. "Over what?"

"I don't know. But this is America. For damn sure I'll

find a lawyer who can tell me."

JOSS STARED AT the mechanical half beast. It was fierce-looking considering it was just a bit of machinery wrapped in fake cowhide. Although the fake bull's head and horns were remarkably lifelike.

"Okay…climb up here—" He slapped the concave slope of the bull's back. "And grab this rope."

Strictly speaking, Troy shouldn't be in the ring with her but nobody at Johnny's was going to tell The Wonder from Down Under that.

Unfortunately they'd drawn quite a crowd.

"Awesome. A Troy Jensen master class," a young guy called from somewhere. Troy gave his admirers a little wave.

He cupped his good hand down low and indicated for her to put her foot in it. Joss did so reluctantly, preferring the safety of the thick foam landing mats beneath her feet. He boosted her like he'd been doing it all his life and she rather inelegantly swung her leg over the beast.

Her skirt was long and flowy with plenty of length and fabric for her to sit astride and not flash half the steakhouse. The excess material between her legs dipped low along the bull's back and she bunched it there slightly just to be on the safe side. It was slippery though and she nearly fell off the other side while getting herself comfortable.

The crowd laughed as Troy grabbed and steadied her. "Jesus, Joss. They haven't even turned it on yet."

"I told you I wasn't very coordinated."

"Well yeah, but I didn't think you meant you couldn't sit without falling off things."

He handed her the rope and she was excruciatingly conscious of his heat as the side of him pressed down the side of her. She was sitting on the bull and he was standing on high-density foam, yet still their heads were even.

"It's not exactly extreme bull riding standard equipment, but it'll do. Grab hold."

Joss tucked her hand under the rope, sitting flush with the bull's back. "Now, grip the bull tight with your thighs." She dutifully tensed her thighs. "Not tense. Grip. Real hard with your whole thigh." His voice dropped, his lips pressing in closer to her ear as he murmured, "I *know* you know how to do that."

A surge of heat shot from her core. Didn't he know she was having a hard enough time sitting on the damn thing as it was without sexual innuendo messing with her equilibrium? She shot him a don't-make-me-get-off-this-thing look but *gripped*.

Hard.

"Atta girl," he whispered.

Joss gritted her teeth. "Don't push your luck, cowboy."

He smiled but eased back from her slightly. "Now, hold your other hand up in the air, palm flat. It's going to provide counterbalance when this sucker starts to spin."

She held up her hand like she'd seen on the TV. "Counterbalance. Check."

"Right. Now when the bull dips forward you need to lean back. When it pulls up, you need to lean forward. Use your hand up there to keep you centered, okay?"

Joss nodded. "Yep. Okay. Got it."

"Think you can last eight seconds?"

Joss was one hundred percent, absolutely, positively certain that she would not. She was even more certain that she'd break something.

Unfortunately, nerves made her mouthy.

"Eight seconds, huh? I heard you rodeo guys had a short fuse. We have pills for that now you know?"

He laughed and his lips were suddenly close to her ear again. "I can go longer than eight seconds as you well know. But even if that were true, I promise you, *doc*, it'd be the best eight seconds of your life."

Great. Now all she was going to think about while a piece of machinery spun and bucked beneath her was riding Troy in exactly the same way. Was it possible to have a mechanical-bull-induced orgasm?

That would be seriously embarrassing.

Certainly more than the good folk of Plainview would have expected from an innocent night out at the Bull Bar. There were *children* watching for the love of Mike.

He chuckled all low and sexy at her scowl before pulling

away again and announcing to the spectators, "I think she's ready, folks."

Joss blushed hoping like hell no one knew just how *ready* she was.

"Good to go?"

She nodded, squeezing her thighs harder, which unfortunately did not help with her pre-orgasmic state.

He winked at her. *Actually winked.* "Ride 'em, cowgirl."

Chapter Nine

Joss's pulse skyrocketed as Troy gave the thumbs-up to the guy operating the switch and the mechanical beast whirred to life. If she had a heart monitor on her now she wouldn't be surprised to see it belting along at a hundred and eighty.

The first pitch forward and back was quite slow but it picked up speed really fast and all Joss could do was shut her eyes, grip her thighs tighter and hang on. And hope like mad she got thrown off before she orgasmed from the friction being created from the rhythmic rub of the bucking bull between her legs.

It was giddying, like a fairground ride as her pulse washed loudly through her head and her breath sawed in and out in shallow pants. The crowd's whooping and hollering came at her from a long way away as the wild pulse built between her legs.

If she didn't have an orgasm she was probably going to have a stroke.

The bull jerked suddenly, her hand was ripped from the rope and she was tossed off in the blink of an eye. One second her ass was firmly seated the next there was nothing but air.

She arced in what seemed like slow motion, her eyes wide open, her brain registering the neon lights, big smiles and wild clapping as garish still-frames.

Her entire body felt alive in those seconds. Pulsing with energy. Tripping the light fantastic.

Joss came to her senses just before she hit the floor. Her self-preservation instincts overriding her pleasure center she tucked herself up into a ball, throwing her hands over her head as she landed on the cushioned comfort of foam mats.

Fortunately not with her skirt over her head.

She lay unmoving for a second or two, getting her bearings, coming back to earth mentally as well as physically.

"*Woot!* Four seconds!" Troy was there, his crooked nose close as he loomed over her, a big, excited grin firmly in place. "I'm impressed. Maybe next time do it with your eyes open?" He squatted beside her and helped her sit up. "How do you feel?"

Well...she hadn't broken anything so that was a bonus. And she hadn't had an orgasm either. Although, who knew what would have happened had she managed to go the full eight seconds.

"Did you like it?"

"I...don't know," she admitted as he offered her his hand and pulled her to her feet.

"You want to go again, right?"

Joss shook her head. *Hell no.* She didn't trust that faint pulse she could still feel between her legs. "I just need some time to analyze it, is all."

He laughed. "You science people think too much."

"Yeah?" She snorted. "You bull riders don't think enough. I can't believe you do that shit for a living."

He nodded, completely unabashed. "*Wild*, isn't it?"

That was one word for it.

Joss's body hummed with electricity. Her skin *crackled* with it. She was aware of the swish of her fringed skirt against her ankles, the scrape of lace against her nipples, the rub of her thighs.

"You wanna go and watch some stars?" They still had over two hours to kill before picking up Damien from work.

He blinked. She wasn't sure if he was surprised at the content of her suggestion or that she'd suggested anything at all. "Sure."

"Good. Let's get out of here."

And she headed for the exit, excruciatingly aware of the man behind her.

TROY FOLLOWED JOSS'S directions. Her mood was more subdued now but there was still an energy about her that was keeping his dick hard.

He knew that feeling.

That post-ride rush could affect a guy in many ways. He could party all night. He could pump iron til he dropped. Or he could fuck like it was his last day on earth.

He preferred what was behind door three. Joss looked like that was exactly the kind of therapy she needed too. And he was more than happy to be the beneficiary of her excess adrenaline if she was looking for someone to help burn it off.

He owed her one after all.

She took him out of town, directing him down back road after back road, twisting and turning and kicking up clouds of dust on the dirt tracks. On the way into town he'd passed land under crops but this landscape was different again, densely populated with forest. "You sure you're not lost?" he asked after twenty minutes.

"Positive. Gus has dragged Damien and I out here about a dozen times this last year. Reckons it's the best spot for stargazing, away from the lights of town."

Troy looked around at the dense forest looming all around him on the dirt track. "It looks like the kind of place serial killers come to bury their victims."

She laughed, uncrossing her legs. She'd been doing that the entire trip. Crossing them and uncrossing them. Like she had ants in her pants.

Or maybe the kind of itch that only a man could scratch.

"Not much longer."

Two minutes later she pointed to another dirt road looming to the left. "Turn here."

Troy turned and in less than a minute they'd come to a clearing. It was a few football fields long and wide and they were surrounded by trees on all four sides. There'd obviously been something here once for the forest to have been cleared back but it wasn't here now, just a big empty clearing perfect for all things celestial, the trees blocking any ambient light.

He drove into the middle of the clearing and cut the engine and lights. There was nothing but silence and the deep black of night.

"C'mon," she said, smiling at him as she pushed her door open. "Let's put the tailgate down and get in the back."

Troy opened his mouth to object but she'd already gone. He smiled to himself as he exited the vehicle. "The back's not exactly clean," he said as he joined her. He carried a lot of his kit in the tray and it tended to smell permanently like bull.

"I don't mind a bit of dirt."

Troy chuckled. That was good to know. It wasn't the kind of dirty he was hoping for though. "I've got a better idea."

It was dark but the starlight was bright and his eyes adjusted quickly noting the ground was well cleared and even. He grabbed her hand and she didn't resist—a fact that tugged somewhere in the vicinity of his heart as he trudged to the front of the pickup.

He drummed the fingers of his uninjured arm on the hood. "Hop on up."

She glanced from his fingers to him, a frown knitting her brows. "Aren't you worried about damaging your hood?"

"Nah. This thing's built like a brick shithouse."

She laughed and it rang clear in the silent night. "You sound very Australian sometimes."

Troy grinned. "Thank you."

"Are you sure?" She slid her hands on to the hood, her knuckles whitening slightly as she tested the strength of the metal. "Mmm," she murmured. "It's nice and warm."

"Which is exactly why it's perfect." It wasn't cold exactly but the night had cooled down and there was the lightest of breezes. "Need some help?"

She waved his hand away. "I got it."

And she did, using his fender to boost her onto the hood, twisting around and sliding all the way back until she was reclined against his windshield. She turned her face toward the heavens and sighed. "This was a good idea."

Troy's gaze wandered up her body. From the tips of her toenails, to the outline of her thighs beneath her slippery skirt and higher still to her pale pink cotton shirt with the five tiny buttons that had been driving him nuts all night.

His gaze lingered on the swell of her breasts. Her ponytail was draped over her right breast and the urge to see her hair out and lose around her head beat like a drum through his blood. Reluctantly his eyes moved further north to the long white stretch of her neck as she gazed above her. It looked soft and vulnerable and kissable.

This had been a *very good idea*.

"Are you joining me or not?" she grouched, lifting her head from the windshield, peering down her body.

Troy didn't need any more encouragement. He shoved his boot on the fender and hoisted himself up, crawling one-handed toward the windshield, turning when he reached his destination and easing himself in beside her, his arm just brushing hers.

It was a perfect night for stargazing. Clear and crisp, the moon not yet risen to obscure any of the stars with its milky glow. A billion pricks of light twinkled down at them from a vast velvet dome.

Neither of them said anything for long moments. Words seemed insignificant in the face of such overwhelming grandeur. Staring at a night sky sure put his puny life into perspective.

It was a different sky to the ones he was used to back home. Different hemisphere, different stars, different constellations. No mighty southern cross. But no less pretty. No less vast.

"Isn't it magnificent?" she whispered finally into the hush.

"It sure is."

"I didn't realize how few stars I'd seen in my life until I moved here."

Troy nodded, his gaze fixed above him. "Yeah. It was the first thing I noticed in the Top End. The skies at night blew my mind. I never knew the meaning of small until then, you know?"

"Yeah." Her voice was hushed as if she didn't want to break the magic of the night.

And it felt magical. Like they were the only two people in the world. Like Adam and Eve. Like whatever happened between them next had already been foretold.

"So, guru." He broke the silence, his voice still low. "Teach me about your American stars."

She laughed and it rang into the night air. "Oh God. I can't remember most of them. The big dipper's up there somewhere. Gus is the enthusiast. You'll have to ask him to bring you out here."

Yeah…Troy really liked Gus but the idea of being out here with him didn't have quite the same appeal.

"He even has a whizz bang telescope for seeing them up close."

The only thing Troy was interested in seeing up close didn't require a telescope. She was right beside him and he preferred to use touch. And taste.

She sighed and it sounded deeply content in the quiet. "I wonder if we'll see a shooting star?"

"Maybe." It felt like anything was possible tonight.

"What would you wish for if we did?"

Troy wasn't sure shooting star wishes should be used for something as base as getting a woman naked so he didn't go there. "Getting back to the circuit as quickly as possible."

She didn't say anything for a beat or two. "What would happen if you didn't?"

"That's not an option." Troy's brain refused to even go there.

"But what if you didn't? For some reason? Humor me."

He didn't see anything humorous about *that*. "My sponsors would be pretty pissed off."

She glanced at him. "You have sponsors?"

"I have three major sponsors." A beer brand, a watch brand and an underwear company. "Each contract is worth six figures."

"*Six* figures?" Joss raised herself up on her elbows, gaping now.

"Sure." He shrugged. "Money can be pretty lousy if you're not winning every stage so sponsorship is important.

She stared at him for a moment or two before lowering herself back to the windshield. "That's…wow."

Troy smiled at the note of astonishment in her voice. "It's another reason why I'm so keen to get back into the extreme tour. The sponsors are giving me some breathing space but it won't last forever."

"I see."

They stared heavenward again, lost in the vastness of space. Troy rolled his head to the side, his gaze falling on her profile. Starlight slanted across her mouth. "What would you wish for if we saw a shooting star?"

She sighed. "To be able to fly."

"What?" He laughed. Troy had expected something more serious. Like a cure for cancer or maybe bringing her husband back. He hadn't expected wings.

If he didn't know better he'd say she was drunk.

"Do you mean growing wings or like a superpower where you can will yourself to fly?"

She appeared to consider the question deeply. "A superpower I think. Wings would get in the way. Plus they'd freak out my patients. Unless I could magically tuck them away somehow and they were all sparkly." Her voice was dreamy as she stared straight up. "That'd be cool."

Troy laughed again. This was a totally insane conversation. He'd thought her sexy as hell watching her ride that bull, tonight. Her lips parted, her eyes closed, a strange mix of fear and something else he hadn't been able to put his finger on. But dreamy Joss, lying under a star-laden sky was a whole other level of sexy.

She waggled her head against the windshield as if to rid herself of the fanciful notion. "God, that sounded mad even to my own ears. Ignore me. I still feel really wired."

"It's the adrenaline."

"No way." She waggled her head again, her denial soft in the night. "I understand adrenaline and this isn't it."

Troy supposed she did. As a doctor she probably knew more about it than he did. She probably understood all the physics and body chemistry behind it.

But adrenaline was something to be ridden, not analyzed.

"Ninety-nine percent of my work is boring mundane stuff," she continued, her gaze fixed skyward. "Colds and flus and fevers. Sprains, strains, broken bones. Gastro outbreaks. And then there's one percent, which is all *go go go*. All life and death with no time to think. You have to respond, to act. Everything you do is critical. Every decision you make is vital. You could power Chicago on the amount of adrenaline running through my system."

Troy watched her mouth move, fascinated by its curves as she talked about an entirely different adrenaline to the one she was currently experiencing. Fight-or-flight adrenaline wasn't the same. He'd been exposed to that plenty in his earlier years. Running from cops, getting into fights, hiding in a cupboard when his father was having one of his drug-induced psychotic episodes.

The adrenaline that had her in its grip was the kind that gave you a high not usually found in legal ways.

"When it's all done it leaves me shaky and strung out. I usually want to barf. But this…" She rolled her head to the side to look at him, their gazes, hooded in the night, locked. "I feel like I could fly right now with or without the shooting star."

Troy nodded. "Great, isn't it? *That's* why I ride bulls."

"Oh no." She shuddered. "I don't ever want to feel like this again. I don't feel in control. If I wasn't so spacey I'd be terrified."

He chuckled at her honesty. "You learn how to manage

it."

"Oh yeah? So what do you bull riders do with it all at the end of the night?"

Troy shrugged. "A lot of guys party hard."

"Do you?"

"Sometimes." The truth was Troy preferred a party for two.

"And what do you do the other times?"

Troy was reluctant to answer on the grounds he might incriminate himself. He'd never been apologetic about his sex life to anyone. He'd slept with a lot of women. They'd all been more than willing to have a wild one-night stand with the Wonder from Down Under and he'd been very grateful for their attentions.

He always used condoms, gave a good as he got and he didn't kiss and tell.

But looking into Joss's eyes under the vast night sky he wished he wasn't bringing that kind of baggage with him. That he was just some regular Joe with a regular past. Not sexual hijinks. Not abuse and addiction and delinquency.

I'm not worried.

That's what she'd told him earlier tonight and the belief behind those words had slugged him hard. He wasn't sure why the hell he'd opened up to her. He never talked about that shit. Until tonight. And her faith in him had been humbling.

He couldn't change his past. For good and ill it had

made him the man he was.

But, for the first time ever, he wished he was…better.

"*Ohhhh.*" A light dawned in her eyes that had nothing to do with the stars and her gaze dropped to his mouth. "So you…"

Troy's breath hitched as her sentence trailed off. "Yes."

She didn't move for a few seconds, just kept staring at his mouth. He was a little worried that she'd actually stopped breathing until the hand that had been lying by her side between them, slowly breached the small gap separating them. Her fingers, cool from the night air, tentatively touched his lips and his eyes drifted shut for a beat or two.

It was the merest of touches—a butterfly wing—but she might as well have shoved her hand down his jeans for the chain reaction that happened in his body.

His dick was achingly hard.

Her fingers slid away and he opened his eyes to find her still staring at him, her fingers resting against the top button of his shirt. His heart thumped so hard, Troy was surprised the bloody thing hadn't popped open.

Hell, he was surprised the entire car wasn't shaking.

Slowly, her hand gathered the fabric of his shirt until she was clutching a handful of it at the base of his throat.

It may have been significantly north of his balls but it felt like she was clutching them instead.

"This is bad," she whispered.

Troy wasn't going to pretend he didn't know what she

meant because he agreed. Even at such short acquaintance he knew that Joss wasn't his typical one-night-stand woman. She had a kid and roots and community. She didn't do this.

She was complicated.

But bad had never felt this damn good.

"I can't remember ever wanting to kiss someone this much," she whispered.

The husky edge to her voice stroked down his spine like the drag of a fingernail. "Then kiss me."

She drew in a shaky breath. "I'm not going to have sex with you."

"Okay." Troy's voice was as husky as hers. He ached to be buried balls deep inside her but he would take whatever crumbs she was willing to throw him.

Already he knew that.

Already he was in way over his head.

Chapter Ten

Troy swallowed as she continued to stare at his mouth, her fingers loosening and tightening in his shirt, loosening and tightening. The tension in the sling of his pelvic muscles cranked tighter, the vastness all around them shrank down to just him and her.

It was too dark to see the moment she made up her mind. One second the heat of her gaze flicked tiny flames over his lips, the next she was yanking on his shirt, extinguishing those flames with the salve of her mouth.

Extinguishing and stoking at the same time.

Her lips slammed into his, hot and urgent, openmouthed and full throttle, charging through his heart and frying every last brain cell in an instant. Fire flashed to his groin and he groaned into her mouth as he slid his hand onto her opposite hip, dragging her onto her side, dragging her flush with him, their bodies joined from thigh to chest, his splinted arm squashed between them.

She kissed with all of her body, deep and wet, making little noises at the back of her throat as she fisted his shirt. She gasped as he thrust his thigh between her legs, breaking the kiss.

"We're not having sex," she repeated, her voice a low mutter as she sucked in air.

Troy's pulse hammered so loudly through his ears he barely heard her. His body was on autopilot, primed to respond to pleasure. To seek it and to give it.

"Okay," he muttered back, his own breath ragged as he palmed her ass.

She leaned in for more, her lips hot and insistent on his, her head twisting and turning as she went deeper, her tongue seeking his, sighing when she found it, moaning when he stroked and probed in return.

The handful of her ass was hot and sweet and he squeezed it reflexively, holding her fast against the thrust of his thigh. She flexed, riding the intrusion. Rubbing lightly at first, then harder.

Dirtier.

Fuck. So hot. So sweet. Like heaven and hell all in one glorious handful.

She broke off the kiss again on a strangled gasp, staring at him, her chest heaving. "We're *not* having sex here tonight." Even as she said it, she rode his thigh harder. Troy's eyes almost rolled back in his head at her barely leashed restraint, at the buck of hips that didn't seem to buy the message her mouth was selling.

"Okay," he agreed. If she chose to dry hump him all the way to orgasm beneath a billion stars he'd be in that.

Hell, he was totally hot for that.

She came back for more. Her mouth moving over his like a storm, fast and furious, lashing him with passion and intensity. She was whimpering now, clutching convulsively at his shirt as her inner battle raged. Like she wanted to push away yet dissolve into him at the same time. Troy clamped down harder on her ass, wanting nothing between them, urging her to keep rocking against him.

She gasped, her lips breaking from his, a low growl of frustration rumbling from her mouth as she moved restlessly against him.

"What do you want, baby?"

He'd asked her the same thing in the bathroom that day because Troy was all about giving women whatever the hell they wanted but also because her conflicted passion bled all over him.

"Not this." Her denial came out on a pant even though her hips were telling him a completely different story.

"Okay. We can stop." It would *kill* him to stop. But he would.

"Are you insane?" she demanded, her voice crazed in the calm of the night as she pushed on his chest and rolled up over the top of him.

Troy sucked in a breath, loud in the stillness, as she rose above him, framed by starlight. He clutched her waist with his un-splinted hand as the apex of her thighs found the hard bulge behind his zipper. Her skirt had ridden up. Legs, bare and pale flashed in the dark as she undulated her hips, rubbing slow and sure along the hard line of his cock.

Her long, low moan sighed into the night, whispering through the trees around them. She looked wild and wanton, and Troy vaulted up, claiming her mouth, sliding his hand into her hair, plucking at the band that held it in its ponytail and releasing it. It fell thick and lush around his arm and in layers over her shoulders and down her back.

Somehow during their passionate make out they'd managed to slide off the windshield to be on the hood proper and he reclined back against it now as she shook her head. The heavy tresses swung free, the celestial backdrop crowning her with a halo of stars.

She was like some kind of creature of the night or forest nymph and he was totally in her thrall, his chest tight, his pulse beating to some wild pagan rhythm.

She swooped down, her hair falling in a curtain around them, blacking out his world as she kissed him again.

And kissed him. And kissed him.

And every time she went to pull away he lifted his head off the hood, chasing, following, hunting her mouth, refusing to let her lips off his.

Demanding more. *Needing* more.

His good hand drifted to her ass and he planted it there, holding her fast against his aching cock, pressing it *hard* between her legs, grinding up as she was grinding down, stoking the heat between their legs into an inferno, whipping the breath in his lungs into a tornado.

"*Yes.*"

She moaned, panting her desire as she pulled away, anchoring her hands on the pectoral muscles of his chest, extending her arms until she was upright. Or, as upright as the length of her arms allowed, anyway. She dropped her head down, hunching her shoulders as she rotated her pelvis, slow and easy.

Her hair obscured her from his view but the rough pants falling from her mouth told him she was enjoying the action. She leaned into him for purchase, her fingers digging into the muscles beneath her palms as she rode his erection. Troy grasped convulsively at her waist as the wild pull in his groin suffused pleasure to the taut bunch of his ass and the tense strain of his thighs.

She pushed away from him, removing her hands as she seated herself fully over his cock. She rode him like a cowgirl at a rodeo, gripping his hips hard between her thighs just as she'd done in the bathroom, just as he'd instructed her to do with the bull.

Gripping hard and grinding harder. Undulating those hips as if she was swinging a lasso about her head.

Her breath came in short, sharp gasps. Her thighs trembled; her head fell back as if she couldn't keep it upright any longer. The tips of her hair brushed his hand at her waist and he itched to wrap it around his fist.

She looked utterly enraptured and she snatched his

breath away.

He grabbed the hem of her shirt instead, his hand sliding under to the feverish flesh beneath. *He needed to look at her.* To see her breasts glorious in the starlight, see her nipples tinged in the first silvery threads of the rising moon.

"Take your top off." His voice sounded alien even to him. Deep as a mine and twice as dark, a crack in the quiet of the night.

Big mistake. The rock of her hips ground to an instant halt. It had been the wrong thing to say. He could almost hear the gears in her brain changing down as she stared at him.

Speaking at all had been stupid.

"Oh God." She groaned, dropping her forehead into her hands as she shook her head. "God...*no no no!*"

Before he could stop her, she'd dismounted and was sitting beside him, skirt askew, legs stretched out in front, face still buried in her hands, her hair an effective barrier from his gaze.

"No," she said, whispering this time.

Troy's head spun as his *body* changed gears from full throttle to hard brake. He waited for a moment or two before he dared speak, before he *could* speak. His brain could barely form a coherent sentence given all his blood was stuck stubbornly south of his belt.

"*Joss.*" He cleared his throat of its husky rasp. "Joss."

"No." She shook her head vehemently and collapsed

against the hood. "We're not supposed to be doing this, remember. We had that one perfect moment. We're not supposed to be ruining it."

Troy's chest was rising and falling as rapidly as hers; their breathing, the only noise, poked holes in the dark as they both shifted air. "I don't think us going at it on the hood of my car is ruining anything."

"I can't have sex with you, Troy."

"Yeah. You've mentioned it once or twice."

She groaned again. "It's just that…you're so damn tempting."

He grinned. At her conflict and the absurdity of it. As if they were teenagers who'd sworn a virginity pledge and had the purity rings to prove it. He rolled up on his side, supporting his head with his palm. "I'm sorry. For being so tempting."

She snorted. "No you're not."

Troy laughed. "You're right. I'm not."

"My life is just fine." She glanced at him, her brow furrowed. "You know?"

Troy did know. But he also knew what it was like to have *more*. "Don't you want it to be great?"

"No." She shook her head. "I'm fine with fine. There were a few years there where fine was more than I ever dared hope for."

Troy understood that too. He'd have given anything for *fine* those first sixteen years of his life.

"But my body has a mind of its own when it comes to you, Troy Jensen. It's been a long time and my libido had decided that you're its kick starter. I could get very distracted by you. Sex would be *very* distracting. And the truth is, I don't have that kind of luxury."

She flicked her gaze to the heavens and he swore he could see starlight reflected in her eyes. Her words found purchase in his heart. He liked the idea that he could distract her because *his truth* was nothing had ever distracted him from his goal of bull riding.

Until her.

"Are you telling me you aren't already distracted? You think *not* having sex is going to stop us from *wanting* to have sex? I don't know about you but I haven't been able to think of anything else but being inside you since your bathroom hand job. Actually…probably since the lug wrench."

It may have been night but Troy swore he could see dull color flooding her cheeks. He certainly saw her knuckles whiten as her fingers twined in the fabric of her shirt.

"It's best just not to go there."

The rasp in her voice told him she'd been there all right. More than once. *Well, okay then.* There was more than one way to skin a cat.

His heart rate, which had started to settle, picked up again. She'd said no sex, then no sex it was. But hell if he'd ever met a woman who needed an orgasm more. Damned if he was leaving here tonight without giving her a bloody good reason to go there as often as possible.

She thought sex with him could be distracting? He didn't need penetration to achieve that. She hadn't even begun to know the meaning of the word.

He vaulted upright and slid off the hood, his feet landing on the ground, the crunch of dirt loud in the silence.

"Troy?"

She lifted her head and glanced down her body. Her skirt was still high and tempting on strong bare thighs that were parted enticingly. His dick, which hadn't exactly returned to its flaccid state, hardened in an instant thinking about how tight her thighs had squeezed his hips.

Wondering how hard they'd squeeze his face.

He grabbed her left ankle and yanked. "*Troy,*" she squeaked as the hem of her skirt flapped higher, the slippery fabric assisting him. Her ass stopped where the hood started to slope into the grill and he bent first her left knee then her right, placing both of her feet on the bumper.

Wide, *wide* apart.

"Troy? What are you doing?"

Her voice shook and he felt it right to the root of his cock. She looked magnificent, sprawled out on his hood, her legs spread wide, her hair spread out around her like some pagan sacrifice under the stars.

He stepped between her parted thighs and his dick shot to granite.

"Troy."

He slid his right hand onto the bare skin of her right thigh, slipping under the hem of her skirt, brushing over the gauzy fabric of her underwear.

"*Troy.*" Her voice was high and strained, the breathy quality of it trailing like vapor into the night air. "I said what are you doing?"

Troy found the thin side strap of her underwear and plucked at it. "What do you think I'm doing?"

"I think you're taking off my underwear."

"I am."

He pulled on it tensing for her resistance, waiting for her hand to clamp on top of his but it didn't. She didn't tell him to stop. She didn't squirm away. She didn't try to pull her skirt down.

She didn't exactly lift her hips either but she certainly wasn't stopping him.

He smiled to himself as he stepped back and eased them down her legs, stuffing them into the back pocket of his Levi's. She shivered as he slid a hand onto her knee and stepped back into the cradle of her thighs.

"I meant what I said about sex."

His hand slid all the way up her leg, pushing what little skirt was still covering her out of the way, holding it in a bunch at her belly button. Her nudity was fully exposed to his gaze and he looked his fill, breathing out hard.

"Who said anything about sex?"

He leaned in, his mouth dropping to the pale slice of

skin between where his hand held her skirt and the thatch of hair between her legs. She wasn't trimmed as was the fashion among the women he usually took to his bed but Troy was *not* a fussy guy and here, under the stars, his head filling with the musky scent of her arousal, au naturel seemed fitting.

The ragged pant of her breathing stuttered into the air as he lazily stroked his tongue down.

Down. Down. Down.

She roused. Shifted. Raised herself up on her elbows, her abs tightening, her thighs tensing. "I think you'll find *that* still counts," she said, obviously throwing one last-ditch effort into denying herself the pleasure she so clearly craved.

He chuckled low, his warm breath fanning her belly, satisfied to feel gooseflesh stippling the soft skin. "If you think this is sex, you need to read some more textbooks, doc."

TROY APPLIED GENTLE pressure to her abdomen where his hand fisted the fabric of her skirt. "Lie back, baby. I'm about to fly you to the moon."

He vaguely heard the quiet *thunk* of her head against the hood as his tongue resumed its southward journey. Vaguely sensed the ooze of tension from her muscles. Vaguely heard her gasp and moan, "Oh my God," as his tongue dipped lower, swiping down the seam of her sex.

Then he was lost to the taste and the feel and the scent of

her. The heat and the wet of her, the salt and the musk, the slick and the sweet. It filled his head, drummed through his chest, gripped his cock. He wanted to tear his zip down and feel her all around him, hot and slick, massaging him, milking him.

But he wanted *this* more.

Wanted to gift her something she'd gifted him in the bathroom—the power of giving without receiving. With no notion of reciprocation.

One perfect moment.

Troy's tongue found the beaded knot of nerves and circled it, pressing hard. She bucked her hips and cried out into the night. So he did it again and again, her hips lifting rhythmically, thrusting into his face with each pass. He lapped it up, circling harder and faster. The reckless demands of her hips, the slickness of her sex, the strangled moans falling from her mouth rocketing his own desire into the stratosphere.

"*Oh God, oh God, oh God.*"

Her thighs clamped tight around his shoulders and Troy could feel them trembling. She was close, *so close* and he wanted nothing more than to rip the splint off his arm, slide both hands under her ass and lift her to him, keep her right where he wanted her as he drove her over the edge.

He grabbed her right leg instead, slinging it over his shoulder, opening her right up, taking full advantage, sliding two fingers into her tight, slick heat as his tongue pounded her clit.

She came then. Hard. And loud. Gasping into the night, her thighs clenching, her internal muscles clamping tight around his fingers, the heel of her right foot drumming into his back.

But he barely felt it. He was too busy with his tongue, flicking at the impossibly hard nub over and over, wringing every second of pleasure out of it. Making her gasp and moan and plead for more.

And he gave more. Gave his all. His fingers thrusting, his tongue circling. He gave her everything until she sagged in his grip and pleaded for him to stop.

He stopped. Slid his fingers out, eased her leg down and dropped his forehead to her belly, trying to catch his breath. Her large abdominal pulse thrummed just beneath echoing the loud thud of his own heartbeat still washing through his ears.

He wasn't sure how long they lay like that, wasn't conscious of anything other than her breathing and her pulse and the scent of warm, satisfied woman. At some stage though her hand landed in his hair and he stirred.

"I think I just scratched your hood up wolverine-style," she said, her voice still a little husky.

Troy chuckled, dragging his forehead off her belly, resting his chin there instead. Her hand fell away and he noticed she wasn't looking at him, her gaze firmly fixed on the stars. "A badge it will wear with honor."

She sighed, long and deep, and Troy wished he knew if it came from pleasure or regret.

"What time do you have to pick Damien up?"

"Soon. But I don't think I can move. I seriously think you melted me into a puddle."

Troy tried and failed not to let it go to his head. There were only two things he was really good at. Riding bulls and satisfying women.

But Joss wasn't just another woman to him. Deep in his bones he knew she was special.

She was the eight-second ride. The gold buckle.

"That's okay. I think you'd make a helluva hood ornament."

She groaned then and flung an arm over her face. "I don't know how I'm ever going to look at you again."

He laughed. So that was why she was studying the sky like an astronomer discovering a new planet. He eased himself back a little, pulling her skirt down to her knees, his good hand resting on her covered thigh.

"Come on, Joss. You can do it," His voice was coaxing as he slipped his hand into hers. "It's not that hard."

She rolled her head from side to side. "Maybe for someone who does this all the time."

He hooted out a laugh at her unintentional insult, not remotely insulted. A bird somewhere beyond the tree line, however, did take objection to the sudden noise, squawking and flapping its wings indignantly.

"You seemed perfectly able to go on after jacking me off in the bathroom the other day."

He pulled gently on her hand. She rose, her hair falling like silk around her head, a dull flush staining her cheeks. Troy's pulse skipped a beat. She was so far removed from his usual type yet his heart swelled just looking at her.

With her sitting on the hood and him standing between her legs, their heights evened out. Her mouth was right there and he wanted to kiss her again. Lie her back again. Make her come again. Make her come all night.

"That was different."

"How?"

"I don't know; it just is," she dismissed. "And how in hell am I supposed to look my son in the eye so soon after you—"

Troy waited for her to finish the sentence. She didn't. He cocked an eyebrow. "Went down on you?"

She blanched. "I was going to say debauched me on the hood of your pickup."

He grinned. "I did, didn't I?"

"Oh God."

She dropped her forehead into her hands again and, before he could stop himself, Troy was pulling her into a hug, the crown of her head pressed into the base of his throat. He half expected her to pull away and when she didn't a feeling of such incredible tenderness swept over him he had to lock his knees against its dizzying effects.

She stayed there for what should have felt like a very long time to a guy who didn't often hug women in a non-sexual way. But it didn't. Surrounded by night and starlight and everything Joss, it felt right.

"So…" Her voice was muffled against his chest and she lifted her head, squirming out of his embrace. "We're even now. That's the end of it. Okay?"

Troy regarded her. She was clearly serious but he wasn't so sure about the prospect. She was a fool if she really thought their chemistry was ever going to be satisfied with a hand job or two. But he didn't want to complicate her life either. If she could keep her hands to herself then he sure as shit could.

"Okay."

She narrowed her eyes at him. "Is that okay like you said about half a dozen times tonight because I wanted to hear it but you ended up having your way with me anyway?"

Troy smiled. "It can be whatever you want it to be, baby."

He slid his hand onto the side of her neck then round to her nape, her hair warm against his fingers as he tugged her close and kissed her. *Hard.*

She kissed him back. *Harder.*

This wasn't the end of it. Not by a long shot.

Chapter Eleven

JOSS ARRIVED HOME from work the following Saturday night at almost midnight. It had been a long, depressing night in the ER. A full moon plus a sizzling summer's day hadn't boded well. She was hot and tired. And hungry. Her feet were killing her.

She wanted food, a cool shower and a deep, dreamless sleep—in that order.

Deep and dreamless… *She should be so lucky.* She hadn't had that since before Troy had debauched her on his hood. Her dreams had been full of erotic images of Troy going down on her in just about every room and on every flat surface in the house.

She was grateful that Troy was away at the Big Spring rodeo tonight. She was at a low enough ebb to consider he may just be an antidote to a heinous shift and she wasn't going there. Thankfully the man was a two and a half hour drive away.

Unfortunately, her plans went awry when she discovered Damien was awake, apparently waiting for her to come home. Once upon a time this would have filled her with motherly pleasure but he seemed tense and broody and an itch shot up her spine.

Tense, broody teen plus tired, emotional mother was bound to end well. *Not.*

Normally Damien would be in bed by now. He'd worked the last few nights until after ten and while he may be fifteen and insistent he didn't need a bedtime anymore, he'd always been an early to bed, early to rise kind of child.

She missed that kid.

He sprang from the couch, hitting the mute button on the remote. The whole house was dark—Gus would have gone to bed hours ago—except for the light flickering from the television.

"You want some sweet tea, Mom?"

Joss blinked, her tired body waking quickly as her mommy senses went into overdrive. "What's wrong?"

"Nothing." He laughed but it was nervous. "Just made up a batch earlier because it's been so hot today and I know how much you like it."

"*You* made sweet tea?"

"Yes."

"Since when do you make sweet tea?"

"It's your favorite." He shrugged. "Thought I'd do something nice."

Five years ago she'd have ruffled her son's hair and hugged him for being such a softie but Damien wasn't the same kid and Joss was a lot more cynical these days.

"Okay." She dumped her bag on the coffee table and crossed her arms, a squall of dread spinning in her stomach. "What happened?"

Damien's face ran the gamut of emotions. Surprise, shock, hurt. Finally anger. "Jesus, Mom." He glared at her, his mouth a bitter line. "Do you always have to think the worst of me?"

Joss shut her eyes briefly, searching for calm. His voice was wounded and it cut her to the quick. Damien was right: she was so tense about him all the time. She did tend to be suspicious about everything he said and did.

She took a deep steadying breath. "I'm sorry," she murmured, her eyes opening. The divide between them yawned wide and she wished their relationship could be like it was before his father had died and he'd turned into the devil's spawn. "I…it's been a long shift. I would love some tea."

"Sit down. I'll bring you some."

Joss gaped a little but sank gratefully into the squishy layers of the couch. Of course she immediately thought about Troy lying shirtless and sprawled on it that first night he stayed and things that had started to relax, tensed again.

Damien re-entered with two long, tall glasses, frosty with condensation. She took hers and gulped half of it. It slipped cool and welcome down her throat but did not, unfortunately, have any effect on the heat between her legs.

"This is very good." She relaxed back into the cushions. There was a fruity flavor to it she couldn't pick. She was about to quiz him for the recipe when he spoke.

"I was wondering if I could..." He swallowed. "Go to a party. Tomorrow night."

And there went her relaxation. Joss sat straighter. "What kind of party?"

"Just a bonfire thing. Out at the Maxwell farm."

Oh no. Joss knew exactly the kind of thing that went on at bonfire parties. If it wasn't the drinking, the pot smoking and the underage sex, it was the yahooing around fields in pickups and the inevitable fights that broke out. Not to mention the hazard of a blazing fire.

"No."

"Mom—"

Joss *thunked* her almost empty glass down on the coffee table. "I said no." She rose to her feet. She was tired; she was *not* going to go seven rounds with Damien over this.

"Why not?" he demanded, also rising to his feet, clearly not caring how tired she was and prepared to go as many rounds as it took.

He was taller than her these days but he was still only fifteen and her responsibility.

"Give me one good reason."

She could give him a dozen but she'd start with the least controversial. "You start work at six Monday morning."

He sneered in a most adult way, his braces bared. "I'm not a little kid, Mom. I can stay up late and still get up early." He stuck out his chin. "What else you got?"

Joss sucked in a breath at his belligerence. In her state it was like a dose of accelerant to what was usually a very slow-burning fuse.

Time to go controversial.

"I don't know, Damien. How about the underage drinking and the pot that will be there and a bunch of drunk, doped-up teenagers piling into pickups all trying to impress each other with burn outs in the fields?"

"You don't trust me," he yelled.

Ordinarily she'd have told him to keep his voice down so as not to wake Gus but once that man was asleep there wasn't a lot that woke him. "You haven't given me a lot of reason to trust you lately, have you?" she yelled back.

"God, Mom!" He gritted his teeth, sucking air in and out noisily, clearly trying to calm down. "I promise I won't drink or do drugs or get into a car with anyone who has, okay?"

"Considering you've lied to me about drinking at parties before, why on earth should I believe you now?"

"Because I'm telling you—" He raised his hand oath-like. "I'm *promising* you I won't."

Yeah. Right. "You think I don't remember what it's like to be young, Damien?" She dropped her voice, pleading with him to try and understand. "To feel bulletproof? To do something rash and crazy without any thought to the consequences?"

"Oh right." Damien's eyes almost bugged out of his head at her. "So *you* were allowed to be young and crazy but I'm not?"

Joss refused to buy into this line of argument. "It's my *job* to protect you from that stuff, Damien. I do not want you ending up like my patient tonight. A *fifteen*-year-old boy, just like you, who's done untold damage to his brain and is probably going to be a vegetable for the rest of his life because he was being stupid in a car with a bunch of his drunk-ass *friends*."

"God, enough with the gross medical stories already," he snapped. "Why couldn't you be a secretary or something?"

Joss had the absurd urge to laugh. She remembered when Damien had been so proud of what she did. "Well I'm really sorry that you got the sucky mother."

"Please, Mom." His voice changed. She recognized the pitch he'd used to get his way since he could talk. He'd obviously forgotten how little it worked. "I promise I won't do anything illegal and I'll be back by eleven."

Joss shook her head. "I'm sorry, Damien. Not this time."

His jaw tightened and his eyes got a familiar glint to them. "Dad would have let me."

She shook her head, already prepared for the jab. "*No*, he wouldn't have." Andy had heard too many of her gross medical stories about partying teenagers to have been blasé about their son's safety. "Trust me on that."

"Yes, he would have," Damien yelled. "You think because you had him for longer than I did that you know everything about him? I knew him too, Mom. And he knew me."

The angst in his suddenly wobbly voice cut her in two and she took a step toward him but he held up his hand, warding her off. "He would have *understood* me. Man to man. I wish you'd died—" He raised his voice even further, hurling the words at her as if he could injure her with their velocity as well as their content "—instead of him."

Joss sucked in a breath and blinked hard at the instant spring of tears to her eyes. He'd said it to her a couple of times in the last few years and it hurt every time.

"And good evening to you both." Joss swung around, startled at the low, calm voice behind her. She hadn't heard the front door open or Troy's pickup. "Looks like we've got some hot heads in the house tonight."

Damien turned immediately to the other man to plead his case. "Troy, can you please tell Mom I won't end up a vegetable at this stupid bonfire party tomorrow night."

Joss narrowed her eyes at Troy. She was prepared to eviscerate him if he so much as looked like he was going to side with Damien.

Troy held up his hands in surrender. "Sorry, mate, but I'm keeping way out of this. I will say though that it may seem a bit of a drag right now but you're real lucky to have a mother who cares what happens to you. Some people don't get that kind of break in life."

Joss could have kissed Troy for his answer. Damien was scowling but she was so damn relieved and happy she'd have jumped Troy for sure had they been alone. The fact he was looking all dusty and cowboy in his hat and Wranglers that sat low on his hips, not to mention his big-ass belt buckle shining in the light from the television, only reinforced this idea.

Not even his splinted left arm ruined his casual sexuality.

"Oh come on," Damien pleaded. "You ride *bulls* for a living. I just want to go to one lousy party."

Joss dragged her head out of Troy's jeans and back to the argument. She knew the only real way to tackle teenage boys was to get down to their level. And what was the one thing that seemed to occupy their mind the most?

Girls.

Dates. Kissing. *Sex.*

Sometimes, you just had to hit them where it hurt. She turned to Damien. "You do know that genitals burn just as well as the rest of the body, right?"

Damien's face screwed up. "Mom! *Jeez.*"

Joss ignored him. "People always think of arms and legs getting burned in these accidents, maybe faces. But never their genitals. Falling into a fire can make a big mess down there. *Big* mess. It can even burn it completely off. No plastic surgeon or medication in the world will ever get it right again."

She saw Troy wince in her peripheral vision at her vivid description.

"*God,* Mom." Damien shook his head in disgust at her

casual use of grotesque medical detail. "You keep on at me at finding some kids from school to hang out with and when I do you go all horror-story-doctor on me. In case it's escaped your attention, there's nothing else to do around this shit-box town."

"You could come to Big Spring with me tomorrow night."

Joss had been prepared to rattle off a dozen things Damien could be doing on a Sunday night, including having some friends over to their place—where there would be no booze, drugs or bonfires—but Troy's offer pulled her up short. They both turned to stare at him.

Damien blinked. "Really?"

"Sure." Troy nodded. "We can watch the show from the bleachers then I can take you back so you can meet the cowboys. I can even take you out to the bulls if you want."

Damien turned to her, no trace of the anger from earlier, or the belligerence. He looked five years old again the day she and Andy had taken him to Disneyland, stars shining bright in his eyes. "Can I, Mom?"

"Uh…sure." She couldn't quite believe how quickly the conversation had turned around but she was immensely grateful to Troy for offering. She glanced at him. "He won't be any bother?"

"Nah." Troy shook his head definitively. "It'll be fun hanging out together—right, mate?"

"It'll be awesome," Damien said, nodding like a bobble

head doll.

"All right then, we leave at three."

Damien grinned like a loon at Troy then loped over to his mother and gave her a kiss on the cheek like he hadn't just cut her heart out and stomped on it. "Sorry, Mom," he whispered hugging her tight before letting her go. "I'd better go to bed."

He shot Troy a big smile and was out of the room in a matter of seconds. Joss stared after him. Love for her son warring with anxiety for him.

"Are you okay?"

Joss turned at the soft enquiry to find Troy had moved closer. Concern jaded his green eyes. "Yes." She nodded. "Thank you for asking. And for offering to take Damien with you tomorrow night."

"He didn't mean what he said, you know."

A lump the size of Texas lodged in her throat as Troy's gaze locked with hers. The fact he understood how wounding Damien's words were made her want to jump him even more. "I know."

His gaze dropped to her mouth for a long slow beat and for a crazy moment, Joss thought he was going to lean across and kiss her.

For an even crazier moment she wanted him to.

"Well anyway…" He cleared his throat and dragged his gaze back to hers. "Better hit the sack myself."

She nodded but he didn't move and Joss held her breath.

One beat. *Two. Three.* She was a nanosecond off grabbing his belt buckle and yanking him closer when he touched the brim of his hat in farewell, stepped around her and walked out of the room.

Air left Joss's lungs in a noisy stream. She hoped like hell Troy locked his door tonight because she owed him big time for what he'd just done for her.

And she didn't trust that she wouldn't go and offer him payment in flesh.

DAMIEN WRINKLED HIS nose. "Man, it stinks round here."

Troy laughed. *Such a city kid.* He even wore the hat Troy had purchased him at one of the merchandising stalls like a city slicker. "Yeah, it's a bit of an acquired aroma."

He remembered when he'd first been in cattle yards as an angry sixteen-year-old. The reek had pissed him off even more, a fact that had slid right off Martin Forrester's back. Troy had preferred the chemical harshness of city smog and diesel fumes to the more earthy odors produced by a herd of bulls and he'd bitched and moaned about it endlessly.

He didn't remember when it had all changed, when the pungent scent of bulls had gone from offensive to invigorating. When it had stopped representing oppression and started to smell like freedom.

He sucked in a huge lungful now as they walked among

the temporary yards constructed to house the bulls for the weekend's rodeo. The smell of beast and sweat and dung and hay and sawdust filled him up and he smiled.

Fucking beautiful.

Damien stopped at a pen and eyed a gray-speckled bull with a white face. The name plate announced him as *Two Up*. "They're big."

"Yep. Mean too. Although this fella isn't full grown yet. The biggest ones can get up to a ton."

"Troy Jensen? Is that you?"

Troy turned and smiled at the woman heading in his direction. Rowan Harper. She worked for her father who was one of the biggest stock contractors in the business. They provided beasts for all levels of the circuit. "Hey, Ro."

"As I live and breathe."

She hugged him tight and Troy let her. She was short and petite with shoulder-length brown hair and one of those faces that looked younger than her twenty-four years. Ro would no doubt still look like a teenager when she was ninety.

She was also one of the few women he'd crossed paths with since he'd become a professional bull rider who'd been stubbornly resistant to his charms. He'd certainly given it a red-hot crack but she'd stuck him firmly in the friend zone.

"Who you got here?" she asked, smiling at Damien.

Damien blinked at the full-wattage smile and Troy smothered one of this own. "This is the son of a…friend of mine—Damien Garrity. Damien, this is Ro. Her dad is one of the stock contractors and what she doesn't know about bulls isn't worth knowing."

Ro's eyes gleamed with speculation, picking up on his slight hesitation during the introduction but thankfully not pressing. She stuck out her hand and Damien shook it on autopilot.

"Damn straight," she agreed, grinning at Damien. "And we at Harper's breed the biggest, baddest bulls around."

Damien grunted something unintelligible, staring at Ro like she was Miss America. Not that he could blame him. Ro might have hidden her figure beneath baggy jeans and men's shirts several sizes too big for her, but she had a face that could render a man mute.

"I heard about your elbow." Ro tapped the splint. "How long you out for?"

"I'll be at Lubbock in two weeks."

"It must be killing you just to sit there and watch."

Troy smiled. "I have been tempted to rip this damn thing off and to hell with it." Although, to be fair, he'd been ably distracted by the no-sex he and Joss Garrity were having.

"Yeah, I figured." She winked at Damien. "He starts to get antsy tonight about competing, you come find me. I know some guys who'll have him trussed up like a turkey, quick as you can blink."

"Yes, ma'am."

She laughed and patted his shoulder. "You want me to show you around?"

Damien's face lit up. "Yes please."

Ro gave them the tour and, for a kid who'd complained about the smell, Damien lapped it all up, asking a bunch of questions. By the time they'd seen all the bulls he was clearly smitten and not just with Ro.

Someone called her name and she acknowledged them with a wave and a quick, "Give me a minute." She turned back to Damien and Troy. "Okay, gotta go. Nice to meet you, Damien and you—" She poked Troy in the chest. "Win some rides, cowboy; want to see you back in the extreme comp."

Troy saluted her. "Tucson. I'll be back at Tucson, mark my words."

THEY MOVED TO the stadium after that. It was a lot smaller than the extreme stadiums but it was no less intense, the fan base no less rabid. There was a reason why bull riding was the fastest growing sport in the country—people loved it!

Damien gawked around him like a kid in a candy store. He stared at the women, cheered at the pyrotechnics and whooped as each bull exploded out of the chute with a rider on its back. He was on his feet for the first bull rider who made it to eight seconds along with the rest of the crowd.

"This shit is crazy," he yelled at Troy over the noise of the crowd.

Troy didn't think his mother would approve of his language but he wasn't the kid's father. Or his conscience. He laughed. "Why do you think I do it?"

Two hours of pure adrenaline-fueled entertainment later and Damien was as high as a kite. Not even one of the bull riders leaving with a busted femur dented his enthusiasm.

"You want to meet some of the guys?" Troy asked as the stadium cleared out.

"Hell yeah."

Chapter Twelve

THEY SPENT HALF an hour in the change rooms, meeting the guys. Damien didn't say a lot but hung on every word and basked in the hero worship directed toward Troy, who was the big fish in the little pond here tonight. For his part, Troy understood what it meant to these guys to spend some time shooting the breeze with one of the ranked riders, so he didn't rush away.

Having one of the big fish tell a rider it was possible to make it to the extreme tour, because he'd done it, could keep a guy going.

Damien turned to Troy as they stepped outside the change rooms. "You're a legend."

There was awe in his voice and he was looking at Troy like he was seeing him for the first time. Not as some guy living over top of his garage who sided with his mom but as some kind of superhero.

"Well, this legend's a little tarnished at the moment."

Damien shook his head. "Doesn't matter. Those guys idolize you."

Troy was about to explain how quickly that could all

turn to shit but he was interrupted.

"Troy Jensen?"

They turned to find a skinny, busty blonde walking their way, hips swinging, bangles jingling. She was wearing a cute straw cowboy hat perched on her head, a tight T-shirt that read *save a horse—ride a cowboy,* a pair of blue boots and jeans that looked like they'd been painted on.

"Oh my God it is you." She smiled big as she reached him and went in for the hug. "I saw you ride in Cheyenne and you got my heart all aflutter."

"Hello there, darlin'," Troy drawled going into autopilot. She pulled out of the hug but kept one hand firmly on his arm.

"It's Sherry." She fluttered her eyelashes. "Whatcha doin' now, big guy? Me and my girlfriends are up for a party."

Troy and Damien glanced over her shoulder at the other three women huddled together all dressed in a similar vein and all smiling openly.

Ordinarily he'd already be pitching a tent in his Wranglers at the thought of four willing women. But Troy—and his dick—had never been more disinterested in his life. It seemed the only woman he wanted to *party* with was more interested in talking herself *out* of having sex with him than succumbing to the screaming tension between them.

"Sorry, Sherry, darlin', I thank you for your kind offer but—"

"It's okay. I'm sure we could find someone for little cutie

here—" She shot a flirtatious smile in Damien's direction. "If that's what you're worried about?"

Troy smothered a smile at Damien's openmouthed expression. She'd just opened the door to every teenage boy's wet dream.

"Sorry, darlin'." He extricated himself from the woman with a friendly smile. "But we have to be heading home."

She relented with a pout and walked away with a, "Maybe next time, cowboy," and a tinkly little wave.

Damien stared after her, his gaze glued to the swing of her butt. Troy reached over and shut Damien's mouth. "You'll be catching flies with that."

Damien turned incredulous eyes on him. "You really *are* a legend."

He said it with such hushed awe, Troy couldn't help but laugh.

"Well, I know what I want to be when I finish school."

Troy laughed again. He wasn't sure wanting to be a bull rider for the chicks was very good motivation. Although, Troy had to admit, it wasn't a disincentive either.

"Women just...*offer* themselves to you?"

Troy shrugged, feeling uncomfortable suddenly with how it must look. The messages that kind of behavior sent to an impressionable young guy.

Christ...since when had he felt *responsible* for anyone other than himself?

"Sometimes," he said, trying to downplay it.

"I wouldn't mind if you took her up on that offer."

"Yeah. I bet." Troy laughed and clapped Damien on the back. "But I'm pretty sure your mother didn't send you here with me to get you laid so let's just get on home now, okay?"

He shrugged as he followed Troy's lead out of the complex. "She wouldn't have to know."

Troy had to give the kid points for trying but he was lousy at subterfuge. One look at the goofy grin a woman like Sherry could put on her son's face and Joss would know for sure his cherry had been popped.

"Trust me, she'd know."

"Okay…fine, but…seriously. If you want to go with them I would totally dig that. I can disappear for a bit."

Troy blinked. Maybe he was just getting more mature but everything about that proposal put an itch up his spine. "Nah, mate. I'm *hanging* with you. And besides…"

His heartbeat kicked up several notches with a sudden jolt, banging hard and fast, drumming loud through his ears. The real reason why screwing four women while Joss's son waited for him in the car didn't do it for him was much deeper than that.

"I really like your mom."

Troy held his breath. He didn't know why he'd said it. He hadn't planned on it. Hell, he'd known her for less than *two* weeks. But the sudden urge to say it out loud had taken hold and he'd always gone with his gut.

And the truth was, he did really, *really* like Joss. But how the hell would Damien feel about the revelation from a man who wasn't his father?

"You having sex with her?"

Troy blinked. Okay…he hadn't expected that. The faint echo of his heartbeat swished in his ears as he consciously chose his words. Not easy for someone who'd never been good with words.

"Well…not that it's any of your business but…no."

The fact that Troy had put his hands—and his mouth—all over Joss, and had thought of little else but being inside her ever since he'd met her, didn't count.

That wasn't the question Damien had asked.

"How would you feel about her being with someone else?"

He snorted. "I say good luck to whoever is crazy enough to try. No man would be stupid enough to have such a…"

Troy tensed for Damien to say *bit*ch. Or something equally unfair. He didn't, but Troy was pretty sure it was what he wanted to say instead of: "Permanently cranky woman in his life."

He breathed a sigh of relief and went on. "You really should go easier on her."

Damien stiffened at the criticism, turning his head to look at Troy. "Why should I?"

A wise man would have backed down but Troy always had rushed in where fools feared to tread. "She's doing the best she can. She loves you and she's trying. It's not easy raising a kid solo, you know?"

"Oh yeah? You raised by a single mother?"

Troy knew where this was going but he let it play out. "No. I grew up with two parents." Neither of whom had given a single fuck about him. Unless he hadn't been able to score for them that day.

"*Your* dad still around?"

"Yep." Last Troy had heard he'd just gotten out of prison—again. God knew how *either* of them had survived this long.

"Well then…" He swung his gaze back to the front, conversation clearly over. "Don't talk to me about stuff you don't know."

Troy thought for a moment or two before he continued, again choosing his words carefully. He didn't want to come across as some overbearing adult who lectured about how good the kids of today had it. But he wasn't going to cut the kid a break on his shit either.

He didn't have to.

"You think if you grow up with a mother and a father that everything's dandy?"

"Of course not," Damien muttered.

"Good. Because two parents can be just as bad as one or none. Yeah, I grew up with a mom and dad but I didn't grow up in a nice house, in a nice street, in a nice small town with nice neighbors and a nice grandfather who opened his home to me. I didn't come from some loving nuclear family.

I grew up in poverty and abuse. In dark corners, slipping through the cracks. Not *one* adult in my life gave a shit about me until I was sixteen years old."

Damien glanced at him. There were two high spots of color on his cheeks. "What happened when you were sixteen?"

"A judge wanted to put me into a juvenile correctional facility."

He blinked. "You went to *juvie?*"

"No. But I nearly did and it scared me shitless." The terrifying prospect of prison had been about the only thing to cut through his numbness.

Damien looked taken aback at that admission. "Wouldna thought a guy who rides angry bulls every weekend would be scared of anything."

"All men get scared from time to time, mate. There's no shame in that. It's how you choose to deal with it that counts."

If he could pass one thing on to Damien tonight it was that. Some things in life couldn't be controlled. But the choices a person made could.

"How'd you deal with it?"

"I was given a reprieve, a second chance, and I took it."

"That's when you ended up on that cattle station you told us about?"

"Yes."

Damien didn't say anything for a moment or two then

he mumbled, "I'm sorry. I…didn't know about all that."

Troy shrugged. "Why would you?" It had been a long time since he'd worn his psychological wounds like a force field, pissed at the entire world. "But if you think your life is really *that* shitty, then you don't know much at all."

"I just…" Damien hunched his shoulders. "She makes me so mad sometimes and…I miss my dad is all…"

"I hear you." Troy nodded. "I get that you're angry. Hell, I *understand* it. Your dad died, and puberty is making Swiss cheese of your hormones and you're living in the middle of nowhere. But boo-bloody-hoo, mate. Cry me a river."

The spots on Damien's cheeks got redder. "Dude. Don't ever go into psychology."

Troy gave a small laugh. "I don't know what those fancy headshrinkers would advise but I do know this, life sucks and it's not fair. You and I just found that out earlier than most. But I'd rather have had a great dad for ten years than a shitty one for all my life. And at least you've still got a *great* mom."

"I s'pose," he conceded morosely. "I just wish she wouldn't talk about dicks getting burned to charcoal in bonfires so much."

Troy winced and adjusted himself at the thought. "Yeah. I'm with you there, mate."

They crossed the parking lot toward Troy's pickup. "You and your mom should come and watch me ride at Lubbock in two weeks' time. Would you like that?"

"Yeah?" Damien brightened. "That'd be awesome."

The conversation veered on to Troy's stats as they climbed into his car and then on to the championships he'd won and the eight-second rides he'd accomplished. Damien asked him about the bulls he'd ridden—the ones he'd conquered and the ones he'd yet to beat—which segued into gruesome injury stories. By the time they'd moved on to best techniques they were at the Plainview town limits.

A sudden hum buzzed through Troy's body as they passed the welcome sign. His muscles tensed, almost cramping but not in an unpleasant way, knowing he'd be seeing Joss soon. He'd told her not to wait up but it wouldn't matter if she was out of sight, curled up in her bed fast asleep, he'd still *feel* her.

Like invisible silk threads weaving strands around his body, drawing him inexorably to her. Strands that grew thicker as each day passed. She felt it too. He knew it. He saw it on her face.

And it was only a matter of time before they both succumbed.

JOSS HEARD TROY'S vehicle pull up outside at almost one in the morning. He'd told her not to wait up but she'd only finished her shift an hour ago and she was too keyed up to sleep. She was dying to know how it went. Whether it had lived up to Damien's Disneyland-esque expectations. Whether he'd behaved himself. Whether he and Troy had gotten along.

A part of Joss desperately wanted Troy to *like* her son. She didn't know why. It wasn't like he was anyone significant in Damien's life. Or hers either, for that matter.

His elbow would be healed and he'd be gone in two weeks for the love of Mike!

But she had been hoping that Troy could be some kind of example for Damien. That her son could look at the successful Aussie bull rider and see with his own two eyes that no matter what shit happened in life, a person could rise above.

That it was never too late to change directions. To make good decisions.

She *liked* Troy—way more than she'd thought possible—and it'd been monumentally hard to stay away from him all damn week. She wanted Troy to like her son because Damien was her whole world and feeling something like this for someone who didn't care for her child would cut her to the quick.

"Hey." She stood as the front door opened. "How was it?"

"Oh, Mom! It was *awesome*."

Joss almost sagged to the floor at the glow on Damien's face and the metal-heavy grin almost as big as the ten-gallon hat sitting on his head. He launched into the highlights without any prompting from her and by the time he'd run out of words her head was spinning.

Joss glanced at Troy. He'd been standing with one hand buried in his back pocket, a slightly bemused expression on his face.

"I guess he liked it, huh?"

He smiled at her. "I'll make a cowboy out of him yet."

The tune to 'Mammas, Don't Let Your Babies Grow Up To Be Cowboys' floated through her head but right now Joss couldn't have cared less about the inherent warning. Her old Damien was back, happy and excited and carefree.

It made her heart sing to see him so animated and engaged. Hell, he hadn't even been this enthused about that stupid party they'd argued over. She didn't fool herself into thinking it would last but for one night it was more than she could ask for.

"Mom. Did you know this guy—" He hooked his thumb in Troy's direction. "Is like this big legend?"

Joss cocked an eyebrow at Troy. "You told him that?"

Troy laughed. "Absolutely not."

"He didn't have to, Mom. Everyone knew him. Like *everyone*. The guys competing and the officials, people in the crowd. Even little kids. I lost track of how many autographs he signed!"

"Really?" Joss sent him a speculative look. "Maybe we *should* have been charging rent?"

"Hey." He grinned. "I offered."

"*And,*" Damien continued, oblivious to the undercurrents, "Troy wants us to go and watch him ride in Lubbock in two weeks. You're not working are you?"

"I'm not working."

Joss couldn't have cared less if she had been. She'd have arranged a swap. Hell, she would have sold her soul. Damien was finally connecting and she wanted to build on that momentum.

Plus how could she pass up a chance to see the legend in action?

"Then we can all go?" Damien's eyes were glowing now. "Together?"

"Absolutely." A sudden thickening in her throat at the word *together* put a dampener on her good mood. "As long as it *is* okay by Troy."

Given her son's current mood she wouldn't be surprised if he'd mistaken something Troy had said. Damien didn't wait for a confirmation from Troy, in two strides he'd scooped her up into a big bear hug. She glanced over his shoulder at Troy, their gazes locked.

"It's a date." His eyes dropped to her mouth and Joss's breath stopped in her lungs.

Damien let her go as abruptly as he'd grabbed her and Joss had to hold on to his arm to stabilize herself. "I'm going to buy some cowboy boots with my savings this week."

Joss blinked. "Okay." This from the kid who had scoffed at all the boots he'd seen around town when they'd first moved.

He turned to Troy. "Thanks so much for taking me tonight. I had the best time."

Troy held out his right hand. "No worries, mate. Anytime." The thickening in Joss's throat became a lump as Damien shook it.

"Well I better go to bed—gotta work tomorrow. I have boots to pay for."

"Night." Troy nodded.

"Night, Mom." Damien kissed her on the cheek and practically levitated out of the room.

Joss stared after her son. *Wow.* "Okay?" She turned to face Troy. She was achingly aware of how alone they were now. Of the way he'd looked at her mouth. Of the way he'd been looking at her since he'd made her come under a night sky in the middle of nowhere.

"Who is that kid and what have you done with my son?"

Troy chuckled. "He did have a good time."

"A good time? *That*—" She hooked her thumb in the direction her son had disappeared. "Is a religious conversion."

Another chuckle, all low and sexy, oozing into the hush of the house and the space between them sweet and sexy, full of unspoken desires. "I think probably women in tight jeans had more to do with it than bulls, boots and God put together."

Joss's pulse spiked. "There were women?"

She hated that she'd asked. That her voice sounded squeaky and unsure. *Sweet baby cheeses.* Of course there were women!

Troy smiled, which did not help the flaming streak of jealousy burning in the pit of her stomach. "Southern women do like them some cowboys."

He was making a joke but Joss's power of reasoning seemed to be broken. The night had turned out better than she'd expected, much better than she'd hoped. For Damien. And that's all that mattered.

The fact she'd been reminded about Troy's life, his reality—autographs and celebrity and *women in tight jeans*—was a good thing.

"Well, thank you." She folded her arms primly. "I appreciate you taking him. I hope he didn't cramp your style."

A small smile played on his mouth but those green eyes were serious. "Jealous?"

"No." She shook her head emphatically.

He cocked his scarred eyebrow but left it alone. "He didn't. Cramp my style. I had fun hanging out with him. It was fun seeing it all through the eyes of a rodeo virgin. Took me back to my first time."

That slight smile was back again as his gaze dropped to the crisscross of her cotton gown, which had been pulled taut by the fold of her arms beneath her breasts. It was too bloody hot for a gown, even a short cotton one, but she'd taken to wearing it since Troy had been in the house and now she wished it went from neck to knee.

He lifted his gaze. "He's a good kid. Easy company. I like him."

And there were the magic words.

Joss locked her knees as a tidal wave of emotions swept over her. Gratitude. Pride. Relief. It was as if Troy had read her mind.

He walked the three paces that separated them until he was close enough to touch her if he wanted. Close enough for her to touch him. Her belly tightened and she dug her fingers into her biceps to stop from doing just that.

"He'll be okay, you know?"

His assurances were like a salve. A balm. They made her feel stronger. Better. Troy had been in some dark places. If he said Damien was going to be okay, she believed him.

"Maybe just pull back on the number of grotesque things that can happen to his junk, yeah?"

She gave a grudging laugh, the tension that had been building in her body evaporating. "Yeah. Sorry…it's an occupational hazard. You wouldn't believe some of the things I've seen."

"Worse than pineapples?"

"Yes."

They both laughed then and the urge to push him down onto the couch and have her way with him got lost in the humor of the moment. It returned as soon as the laughter dissipated but she took a step back, in better control of herself now. "Well thank you, again."

He eyed her for a beat or two like he might take a step closer, try and reclaim the moment, but he didn't. He just nodded slowly and said, "No worries. Good night, Joss."

Joss stood aside. "See you in the morning." And held her breath as he brushed by.

Chapter Thirteen

THE BOTTOM STAIR creaked under her foot and Joss froze. She didn't dare even breathe. It sounded like someone had felled a tree and it had crashed through their fence. Her pulse tripped along at a frightening pace. She waited for the house lights to spill into the backyard. For Gus and Damien to charge through the door and demand to know what the hell she was doing.

But nobody came. No lights turned on. It was just her and the night and her fibrillating heart. She breathed again, almost tempted to turn around and go back to bed. Forget this crazy idea and take the edge off her frustration the old-fashioned way. But after tossing and turning for the last hour, she didn't want to go back to an empty bed.

She didn't want to deny herself any longer.

She needed it, damn it. She was a grown woman. With a grown woman's appetites. Being a widow and a mother did not make her sexless.

And Troy wanted her. She knew it on the roadside that night with the lug wrench. She knew it in the bathroom that day. She knew it on the hood of his car under the stars. And she sure as hell knew it tonight when he'd brought her son home after giving him the time of his life.

Yes, he was younger than her. Yes, he was a drifter. Yes, he'd be gone in a couple of weeks. But it was just sex. She wasn't going to his room at two in the morning to get down on bended knee.

Well…not in the proposing marriage way anyway.

Joss took a steadying breath and tiptoed up the remaining stairs, the moon lighting her way. Her heart was beating even faster as she reached the small landing at the top and it wasn't from exertion. Her hands were trembling so hard she could barely knock. Considering how loudly her heart was banging she wondered if she even needed to.

But knock she did. Quietly…

Then, nothing. No acknowledgment. No covers rustling. No footsteps. She was conscious of the tip of her ponytail swishing against the middle of her back as she laid her ear to the door, straining to hear *anything*.

But there was nothing. Just the insects and her heartbeat as she straightened and stood in a quagmire of indecision.

For the love of Mike, what was she doing? Why was she here?

She glanced down her body. *What was she wearing?* She'd ditched the gown for just her spaghetti-strapped tank top and boxer shorts. Probably not what one of his *buckle bunnies* would wear to a seduction…

But she didn't own sexy underwear or satiny negligees

anymore. And even if she had, she didn't have any moves to go with them.

God. What was she doing? She had *no* game at all.

Humiliation and thwarted desire twisted inside her as the door remained stubbornly closed and Joss conceded it wasn't going to happen. She wouldn't knock again.

She had *some* pride.

If the man could sleep like the dead with all that frustration built up inside him then maybe she'd been mistaken about how much he wanted her. Maybe he just wasn't that into her and she'd been mooning over him like some poor, desperate, sex-starved widow.

She cringed at the thought and turned away, taking a step just as the door opened.

"*Joss?*"

A surge of overwhelming relief at his whisper made her snippy. "Jesus, you took your time."

Her whisper was more like a hiss in the still of the night.

"You have any idea how hard it is to get into underwear one-handed?"

Of course the man slept naked. Why wouldn't he?

Her eyes traveled over acres of bare skin kissed by moonlight save for the hard plastic of his splint and the cotton strip of underwear that clung to hips and thighs and hugged his package like they'd been tailor-made.

With supreme effort she dragged her gaze up to his face. His jaw was stubbly and he had a mark on his cheek, which she figured was from the bedclothes. He was a tall, lean streak of cowboy and, as an honorary *southern woman*, she *did* want her some of that.

She took a deep breath and recited what she'd practiced on her way up the stairs. "I'm assuming your legendary status extends to the bedroom?"

His gaze ran over her just as thoroughly. Goose bumps broke out in its wake, dusting her skin from top to toe, pebbling her nipples into hard achy points. He stared at them the longest and she almost moaned on his doorstep. His gaze returned to her face and he regarded her with slumberous eyes for several drawn-out beats. "Tell me what you want."

Joss's breath hitched. *He didn't know?* "I want to…have sex with you."

He shook his head. "The specifics, Joss. What do you want right now? What do you want *first?*"

This wasn't how she'd fantasized it would go down and she'd fantasized about it *a lot*. She hadn't expected him to just stand there, stripping her naked with his eyes, *doing nothing*.

Waiting for her to tell him what she wanted.

She'd thought he'd take control. Had *hoped* he would. She was rusty at this seduction business after all. But his bluntness was a surprise turn-on, cranking the exquisite burn of desire between her legs.

It made her shaky and wet and her nipples tingled. *It*

made her bold.

"I want you to rip my top off and suck my nipples." She sucked in a ragged breath. "That specific enough?"

Not so rusty after all.

The long slow bob of his Adam's apple in the moonlight was gratifying as he grabbed her arm and dragged her inside.

The heat and the soapy aroma of him surrounded Joss as he backed her against the door. He didn't rip her top off. He didn't do anything for a moment. Just looked at her. Then, very slowly, very surely, he slid her tank top up, his thigh slipping between hers just as slowly, just as surely. He pushed it up until it was just under her neck and his thigh was wedged high and hard.

Her breath hitched and her nipples, already unbearably taut, puckered to agonizing points, screaming for relief. Part of her wanted to cover up, afraid her B cups may not compare to younger, perkier breasts but the other part wanted to thrust them out in silent invitation.

"Jesus," he whispered, his gaze devouring the sight of her. "You're beautiful."

It had been such a long time since anyone had called Joss beautiful and she wanted to cry but then he bent his head, his hot mouth closing over the hard tip of one breast and it was a different noise wrenched from her throat.

Not a sob. Not a quiet whimper or a low keening moan. *Not ladylike.* It was a guttural, primitive bellow.

The sound of a woman who hadn't had her breasts

touched by a man in a *very* long time. A woman whose breasts had always been exquisitely sexual.

"*Shhh, baby,*" he whispered against her mouth, kissing her quiet, kissing her long and sloppy before breaking away again and bending his head to her other breast.

She came back to herself. Aware of who she was and where they were. Aware that her son and father-in-law weren't that far away and she'd probably just roused the entire neighborhood. She bit back the next primitive noise pushing against her vocal cords for release, gasping and moaning into his shoulder instead, sinking her teeth into the big rounded ball of it as he pinned her to the door with the wedge of his thigh and the flat of his tongue.

Sucking and licking and swiping, grazing her nipples with his teeth, pressing his thigh hard between her legs until she was so close to orgasm she could barely stand upright.

"Stop," she said, wrenching his head from her breasts, panting for breath and sense. This time she wanted him to be inside her when she climaxed.

She wanted them to come together.

"What now?" he asked, his eyes glazed, his voice raspy with desire.

The words rushed to her tongue. Graphic, descriptive, dirty. *I want to ride you like a cowgirl.* But she couldn't say them. She wasn't a woman who hung around rodeos hoping for some cowboy action—she was an ER doctor for crying out loud.

"Tell me," he whispered, hot in her ear, the fingers of his right hand trailing across her chest, around a nipple, down her belly.

Her eyes fluttered closed. His fingers breached the waistband of her boxers.

"You can say it."

They found the band of her underwear and the muscles directly below clenched tight. *Oh God.* She clamped her hand on top of his, opened her eyes. "You," she murmured. "On your bed. Inside me."

Slowly he eased his thigh away. Joss whimpered at the loss as he picked up her hand and gently tugged, pulling her away from the door. He walked backward, unhurriedly, his eyes glued to the bounce of her exposed breasts, looking his fill. Joss trembled beneath his stare, enthralled by the look in his eyes.

The room may have been dark but her night vision was excellent.

The backs of his knees hit the bed and he stopped. Sat. Sunk back onto his good elbow, his splinted arm resting across his abs. His hot, hungry gaze traveled from her knees all the way up.

"Take off your clothes."

Oh God. Oh God. Oh God. It'd been four years since she'd been naked in front of a man.

"Joss?" He levered himself upright, his hand sliding up the back of her thigh, stopping halfway, his thumb stroking.

His gaze moved from her breasts to her face. "I want to see all of you."

Joss nodded. She wanted him to see all of her too. She wanted to see *all* of him. It didn't stop her hands trembling as they crossed over and yanked her top all the way off, nor her thighs quivering as her thumbs hooked into the sides of her boxers and underwear. He slid his hand away so she could push them down and off as one.

She was sure he'd been with women who made stripping in front of a man a work of art. A tease. An integral part of foreplay. That wasn't her. She was relieved she didn't land on her ass as she'd kicked her ankles free.

"*Joss.*"

He stared at her, his gaze raking her from head to foot, a hot wave of pleasure rippling through her belly as he leaned back on his elbow again. His eyes lingered on her unbearably taut nipples and the apex of her thighs, already slicked with her arousal.

"Do you think you could do the honors?" The huskiness of his voice flooded her pelvis with sensation, as potent a stimulus as his tongue on her breasts.

He wanted her. She could *hear* it.

He lifted his hips off the bed slightly. "It took me long enough to get into these bloody things."

Joss's gaze was drawn to his underwear. To the erection stretching the fabric to the limit. Her knees almost buckled at thought inside her.

She planted a knee on the mattress, stroking her fingers up the lean muscles of his thighs to the waistband of his underwear and tugged. He lifted his hips as she peeled them away and she stood again, looking down at him in all his glory.

"*You're* beautiful," she whispered, her gaze snagged on the rigid perfection of him.

Joss had seen a lot of penises in her life. It was an occupational hazard and, as such, she tended to view them through the lens of a doctor. They were functional organs. Blunt and harsh and efficient. Practical but dangly and…primitive.

Ugly even.

Not something that inspired art or poetry. Not pretty.

She'd been dead wrong.

Troy Jensen's cock was *beautiful*. Long and lean like him, lying taut and primed against his belly, the head in perfect proportion, a slender vein full and bulging along the length of the shaft.

He chuckled low. "I think that's the first time anyone's ever called it that."

She supposed a more practiced woman would have used sexier language. Big. Huge. Mighty. Or other grandiose terms. But she called it like she saw it.

He crooked his finger. "Come here."

Joss's breath heated in her lungs but she stayed put. She needed to think now because as soon as she got on that bed, she didn't want to think again.

Just feel. Let herself go.

"Condom."

She'd been on the pill when Andy had died and had stopped taking it. Her one-night stand had used a condom. Frankly, she wanted nothing more than to feel all of him, inside all of her. But what kind of doctor would she be if she didn't practice what she preached?

"Wallet." He pointed to the bedside table.

Hands shaking, Joss leaned over and extracted the foil packet tucked into one of the credit card slots. She held it up, looking at him, at the desire in his eyes and the hard, potent jut of him.

She hesitated. "I'm—" Her voice cracked and she cleared it. "I'm not going to last very long, I'm afraid."

He chuckled again. "Hey, you're talking to the eight-second guy, remember?"

She smiled but it was short-lived as she tried to articulate what she needed. "Can I just..." She petered out, her cheeks heating as she dropped her gaze to her feet.

How could she even ask for that? Speak it out loud?

"*Joss.*" His voice was low but insistent and she glanced at him. "*Anything*. You can have anything. What do you want?"

She may have had him by seven years but she felt like an ingénue standing before him. "I want to..." God! Her pulse tripped madly through her temples. "I *don't* want to...go slow. I don't want foreplay. If you kiss me I think I'll explode into a thousand pieces. I'm too achy and trembly and needy…"

Sweet baby cheeses. She was screwing this up. "I don't think I can contain myself. I just want to…"

His hot gaze bored into hers. "You just want to *fuck?*"

God yes, *that*. The way that word rolled off his tongue like it had been invented especially for him. "Yes." She nodded. "I need to feel you in me. *Now*. I just want to…put the condom on and…sink down on top of you until you're so deep inside I can barely breathe."

His right hand slid onto his cock, gripping the shaft. "You want to ride me, darlin'?"

Joss's cheeks turned crimson but she couldn't look away. He spoke so plainly and touched himself with such ease. Such boldness. It turned her on and he knew it—and that cocky young cowboy was just what she needed right now.

Still she didn't trust her voice. Didn't trust that she wouldn't beg. Or possibly whimper. She just nodded.

"Then hop on board."

Hop on board. Every nerve cell in Joss's body fritzed out at the casual suggestion. Just, *hop on board*. Then the realization it really was that easy filtered through and her system sparked to life.

Joss fumbled with the condom, tearing it open with shaking fingers as she put her knee back on the mattress followed by the other one, spreading her legs as she caged his thighs between hers. She was excruciatingly aware of the mad tingle of her arousal. Of her wetness.

He angled his erection up for her and her mouth watered. She wanted to taste it. Touch it.

Later...

She placed the condom over the head and he rolled it on. "All yours, baby," he whispered, his hand sliding to her hip, urging her closer.

Joss shuffled closer, her gaze locking with his as she grabbed the base of his erection. He sucked in a breath but she barely heard it as she aligned herself. She gasped as the hard nudge of him slid along screamingly sensitive flesh.

"Yes...baby." His gaze heated as his hand tightened on her hip. "Just there."

It *was* just there. And it felt good. *So good.* Hard and full, notched at her entrance.

It felt better when she flexed her hips to take more of him, just one flex and she was sinking down. Slowly, so slowly, all the way down.

He groaned as she took him to the hilt. A low, continuous guttural noise that wrapped around her, stroking rough fingers down her spine. "Joss," he whispered, his hand gripping and releasing her hip. "*Jossss.*"

Her name sounded like a benediction on his lips, filling her heart as she bottomed out on a low moan. Her back arched as she adjusted to the intrusion, absorbing the long-forgotten feeling of being stretched and full.

Reveling in it.

Suddenly boneless, her neck lost the ability to hold her

head upright and it fell back, her eyes fluttering closed.

"You're magnificent," he said.

Joss roused to his words, trying to pull all the scattered parts of herself together as the pulse low in her body craved more.

Craved friction and movement. Craved completion.

But her bones felt like lead, her brain like custard and in the end, it wasn't her who moved, it was him. He curled up, his hot mouth closing over one of her nipples, and she cried out, her internal muscle clamping hard around him as the lead in her bones melted to marshmallow.

His good hand reached behind her, tugging her ponytail, keeping her head tilted and her back arched, presenting her breasts to him on a platter. He flexed his hips, withdrawing a little, her protest moan quickly smothered by a gasp at his re-entry.

It was a perfect thrust. The perfect angle. And he did it again and again, pumping in and out with slow deliberate strokes.

Joss wasn't exactly doing the riding but she was beyond caring as he picked up pace, hitting the right spot over and over, twisting the tension inside, cranking up the heat, pulling things tighter and tighter. Her heart crashed and her lungs grabbed for air as she sunk her nails into his shoulders for purchase.

His mouth moved to her other nipple and her orgasm was on top of her, flaring from the base of her spine and rippling through her thighs and abs and glutes. Her head snapped up as it coalesced in one cataclysmic implosion.

"*Troy!*"

It was desperate and needy, more a cry for help than anything else because in that moment the pleasure overwhelmed her. It swamped her in heat and silk and electricity until she feared she would drown in its intensity.

He released her nipple, seeking her mouth. "I know, baby," he muttered against her lips. "It's okay, I've got you."

And he did. He had her. Kissing her greedily through the maelstrom, holding her tight as he rocked her higher and higher, swallowing her gasps and cries, just as she swallowed his when he joined her in the rapture.

Their frantic hearts beating as one.

Chapter Fourteen

Troy checked his rearview mirror for the hundredth time since they'd hit the road this morning. Damien, who'd read everything rodeo he could get his hands on since Big Spring, was sitting shotgun, reciting some stats. Troy was only half listening, eyes fixed on the tiny glimpse of Joss who was driving the car behind. He'd just lived through the most intense eleven days of his life with her and it felt odd to be so far apart.

They'd decided to take both vehicles to Lubbock for convenience of getting around and because his pickup, while it could technically sit three, wasn't ideal for two full-grown adults and a practically fully grown teenager especially on a longer trip. Although Troy wouldn't have minded been squashed up against Joss.

He'd have found it difficult keeping his hands to himself though, which would have been a problem with Damien in the car. God alone knew how he was going to keep his hands off her at the hotel for two whole nights after having an all-access pass for the last ten.

He'd stupidly insisted he'd get a room big enough for

them all to bunk in together when Joss had said she'd book a separate room. He'd wanted to create a shared experience for them all. Damien had been excited about this trip for two weeks, excited to be hanging out with Troy and Troy was happy to indulge him.

But he should have thought it through a bit more.

They'd have no privacy now. At least with a second room it opened up a few more possibilities. Like her sneaking into his room once Damien was asleep.

Like she'd been doing the last eleven nights.

He flexed the fingers of his left hand around the steering wheel, reminding himself how inappropriate it was to be thinking naked thoughts of Joss while her fifteen-year-old son sat not three feet away. But it had been hard to think of anything else since that night she'd knocked on his door.

Knowing she was coming to him the next night and the next night and the next had kept him in a permanently heightened state that not even working shoulder to shoulder with her father-in-law had been able to dampen.

Determined to banish the thoughts, he gripped and released his fingers experimentally. His left arm had been aching a little since Joss and the PT had given the all clear to take it out of the splint yesterday—not that he'd admit it to either of them.

He was still not used to seeing his arm out of the bloody thing, its paleness strange next to the nut brown of his other arm. It felt strong though, despite the ache and, thanks to sticking squarely to his exercise regimen, he had almost full range of movement through his elbow.

There were some more investigations he'd have done once he was back on the extreme circuit but for now he was just pleased to have full use of his arm back. For bull riding *and* for other kinds of activities.

Like being able to slide both hands onto Joss's ass last night. Being able to palm a breast in each hand. Being able to support himself on both elbows as he'd sunk into her and pushed them both into the abyss.

And...he was back to naked Joss again.

THE MOTEL WAS the standard, basic motel that fit the budget of most pro circuit riders. Troy had wanted to book a hotel in the city heart but Joss had insisted that they stay wherever he normally would so they'd ended up where most of the cowboys were staying.

But he had booked their best room—a suite.

The *suite* wasn't exactly up to the Waldorf's standards but she didn't seem to mind as she surveyed the room—and given that Troy would have more than happily slept in his pickup, a bed was a luxury.

This room had three.

A queen, a single and a couch that converted to a bed.

He glanced at the queen bed longingly then at Joss who

chose that moment to look at him, longing in her gaze too. They didn't say a word; they didn't have to. Her eyes roving over him in a long slow lick said it all.

His dick twitched. He was going to miss her tonight.

"Let's go get something to eat," she announced, dragging her gaze away.

"Yes please," Damien said, oblivious to the undercurrent. "I'm starving."

Troy was starving too but not for anything he could order off a menu. It was going to have to wait though. Until after the weekend. Until they returned to Plainview.

But he hoped she knew he wouldn't be letting her out of his bed until he'd eaten his fill.

They found a steakhouse in the main street. Troy and Damien loaded up with ribs and rump while Joss stuck to a Cobb salad. They chatted as they ate, mainly about tonight's event. Damien steered the conversation, which at one stage was interrupted by a customer who had recognized Troy and wanted an autograph for his kid.

"See, Mom." Damien nudged her. "*Total* legend."

"Total," she agreed, a small knowing smile parting her lips as her gaze ate him up.

Troy's dick did more than twitch this time: it went to full boner in seconds as he imagined pushing it between those wicked lips.

"Can we get cobbler?" Damien asked.

Troy ordered peach cobbler in a voice that hopefully did

not betray the slew of dirty thoughts running through his head all involving eating cobbler off Joss's body, which did not help the erection situation.

She shook her head at both of them as they finished their desert and Troy immediately ordered a huge ice-chocolate each to round the meal off.

"I can't believe you guys can possibly fit another thing in."

"Easy," Damien said, burping loudly then laughing at his effort.

Troy locked his gaze with hers. "I have a *big* appetite."

"Yes." Her cheeks pinked a little.

Yes *indeed*. She knew that *intimately*. "I'm very hard to satisfy."

She knew that too. No matter how much naked time he spent with her, it was never enough. Her cheeks pinked *a lot* as her gaze slid to her son who was studying the menu, then back to him.

"I've noticed."

Considering he kept finding ways to keep her in his bed each night, it'd be hard not to.

"Hey, Mom, did you see all these different ice teas they have? You should get one of those."

She held Troy's gaze for a beat or two before turning her attention to Damien. Troy adjusted himself under the table. It was going to be a long three days.

WHEN THEY GOT back to the hotel Joss headed for their room with Troy following close on her heels, his gaze glued to her ass.

"Oi," Damien called.

Troy stopped and glanced over his shoulder. "You oi'd?"

Damien grinned. "You said you'd shoot some pool with me in the games room."

Fuck. He had? *Jesus.* He didn't remember. His brain had suffered from a severe lack of oxygen for at least fifty percent of their time at the steakhouse so he wouldn't be surprised. He sighed. He had a few hours to kill before he had to be at the arena and he supposed playing pool beat the mental torture of having to watch Joss in the same room with *three* beds and not being able to lay her on any of them.

"Right, sorry. Yes."

"You want to come too, Mom?"

Troy glanced at Joss hoping like hell she'd decline. He only had so much self-control and watching her bend over a pool table with her legs parted would be testing his outer limits.

"Nah." She shook her head and smiled at her son. "You guys go on and have some fun." She flicked her gaze to Troy. "I think I might have a shower. Wash my hair. Shave my legs."

Troy narrowed his eyes as his erection returned to full

mast. She was *so* paying for that.

IT TOOK TROY an hour to extract himself from the games room. There was some kind of irony that salvation finally came in the shape of a girl.

Damien's eyes had stuck out on storks the second she'd entered the room with her two brothers and it had taken little maneuvering on his part to get them all introduced and teaming up. Damien didn't object when Troy made a lame-ass excuse about equipment checking.

Hell, Damien barely looked up from the girl.

It took Troy less than thirty seconds to be standing at the door to their hotel room.

Have a shower? Wash her hair? Shave her legs?

Man he'd played the lousiest pool of his life imagining her all wet and slippery. In fact his hands were shaking so hard it took three goes to slide the key card correctly into the door.

He almost kissed the bloody thing when it finally flashed green and the lock whirred open. The door gave under his shoulder and he pushed it inward to find an empty room. His dick, however, as stiff an insistent as a divining rod, knew exactly where to find her.

He stopped only to put the chain across before he crossed the room, yanking his wallet out of his back pocket as he went, fishing out a condom before tossing the thin fold of leather on the ground near the bathroom door.

He didn't doubt for a moment the closed door would be unlocked and he didn't bother to knock. He just yanked it open, his pulse thundering, catching her as she stepped out of the shower, her wet hair hanging in damp strips over her shoulders and down her back, a towel wrapped securely under her arms.

She startled slightly before letting out a shaky breath. "Troy."

He pulled the door shut. Locked it. Threw the condom on the vanity. Reached for the tail of the towel secured at her cleavage and tugged.

It fell to the floor.

She didn't cover herself. She didn't tell him to get out. She just returned his hungry gaze, the tempo of her breathing as ragged as his.

"Christ." He grabbed her arm and hauled her close, his hands landing on her ass. "I missed you." He'd been inside her less than twelve hours ago but knowing it was going to be another two days until he got to be with her again made him crazy.

He turned her, pressed her into the wall next to the vanity and kissed her, deep and hard. Kissed like he hadn't kissed her in the longest time, one hand urging a thigh up, the other tangling in her wet hair.

"Wait, stop," she said, panting heavily as she placed a

hand on his chest. "Damien?"

"Playing pool," he dismissed, dipping in again to reclaim her mouth.

"Which means he could be back any moment."

"Trust me, he's with a girl. He won't be back anytime soon."

She blinked. "A girl?"

"A very cute teenage girl with two brothers in tow. She's fifteen; they're seventeen and eighteen. They're visiting from Florida. Good enough?"

"I suppose."

She supposed? "I've just played some of the worst pool in of my life thinking about you in this bloody shower so if there's anything else, speak up now, because next time I kiss you, I'm not stopping."

She smiled. "Don't you have some kind of rule about no sex before a ride?"

Troy laughed. Her voice was light and teasing and his heart just about melted out his toes. "Honey, do I look like some dumb jock to you?"

He didn't give her a chance to answer, just picked right up where he left off, swooping in to claim her mouth, groaning as her tongue greeted his.

Her hands got busy then. Really busy. Somehow his shirt was off and his zip was down and her hands were inside his jeans, pulling his erection out, squeezing it, palming it.

"God," he muttered, leaning in to her, pressing his forehead to the tiles beside her head, panting hard. "That feels so good."

"Bet I can make it feel better."

Her breath was hot on his neck and he laughed as she groped beside them for a moment before producing the condom, tearing it with her teeth and rolling it on.

"Lift me up."

Heat flared in Troy's groin—he didn't need to be told twice. He slid both hands to the groove where her ass met her thighs and boosted her up the wall until the head of his cock nestled into the slickness between her legs.

Her wet hair was plastered against her neck and her chest and even the tiles behind her. Her cheeks were flushed and her mouth was red and full from their kisses. She took his breath away.

"God you're sexy," he said, leaning in to kiss her quick and dirty before whispering, "Hold on, baby."

He thrust then, a decisive buck of his hips, pushing all the way to the hilt, kissing her to smother the cry ripped from her throat. Kissing her until she was moaning and she'd relaxed around him.

"You okay?" he murmured.

She didn't answer for a beat, just locked her ankles around his ass. "Again."

Troy withdrew almost all the way and thrust again, her head bumping against the wall, her breasts bouncing enticingly. His mouth watered at the sight.

"God yes." She rotated her hips. "Again."

He went again, bending his head to a nipple. She gasped and arched her back in invitation and he switched to the other breast as he withdrew and thrust again.

She arched her back more, bowing right off the tiles, wrenching her nipple from his mouth, forcing him to take a step back. Just her head and shoulder blades were pressed into the wall now, the lock of her ankles and the thrust of his hips the only thing supporting the rest of her body.

Troy had never seen a more magnificent sight. Her body strung taut between him and the wall, his big hands branding her hips as he thrust in and out, her breasts jiggling with every pump, her nipples dusky-pink and steepled in arousal. He dropped his head to one and she gasped, sinking her hands into his hair and holding on tight as he rolled it around his tongue.

She held him to her all the way to the end, pulling him off occasionally and dragging his head in the direction of the other nipple, demanding with nothing more than an urgent whimper that he service that one too.

And Troy was more than happy to oblige.

He met every one of her demands, not lifting his head, just sucking and thrusting, sucking and thrusting, harder and faster and more urgent as heat and tension and sensations built deep inside his belly, twisting and pulling.

Troy's legs shook and his chest was too tight for his lungs and his pulse hit stroke levels as the first, "*Yes!*" was ripped from her throat, her internal muscles clamping around him as she bucked in his hands.

He gripped her hips tighter, thrust harder, flicking his tongue quicker over the taut peak in his mouth as his own orgasm boiled from the depths of his balls. It seeped into his ass and the backs of his thighs and the bundle of nerves at the base of his spine, shooting down to his feet and all the way to his skull.

"Ohhhhhh God," he muttered against her breasts as everything inside him imploded and his knees threatened to buckle. But he didn't stop. He didn't stop licking and sucking or thrusting and pounding, stoking their orgasms, wringing every last ounce of pleasure out of it.

He didn't stop until he was spent and Joss was limp in his arms.

"I sure as hell hope that girl is as cute as you reckon because I'd hate to have to explain the noises coming from the bathroom to Damien if he's just outside."

Troy chuckled, kissing the side of each breast. Red blotches covered her chest from the scratch of his whiskers. A possessive streak he didn't know he owned rumbled appreciatively inside him at having marked her.

He shifted slightly, boosting her back up the wall, pinning her there with his chest and the intimate join of their bodies. He pressed his face into her neck, trying to settle his spinning head and catch his breath.

He inhaled the clean soapy scent of her skin, a feeling of

utter contentment settling over him. "I think I'm falling in love with you, Joss Garrity."

She laughed, her body still pliant and relaxed against his, obviously amused by his confession. "I'm pretty sure that's endorphins not love."

Troy laughed too. It was totally mad but he couldn't shake the feeling that had been building since he'd first met her on the roadside. "I know it sounds crazy."

"It's just the sex talking." She kissed his temple.

"Nah." Troy dragged his forehead from her neck, capturing her gaze with his. "It's not. I've had a lot of sex. This is different."

It *wasn't* something he'd said on a whim. Or hell…maybe it had been but the sentiment behind it was real this time. It wasn't coming from his balls.

It was coming from some other place deep inside him.

It felt like he was a jigsaw piece finally finding the puzzle to which he'd always belonged. He'd never really fit anywhere. Not at home trying to make himself simultaneously small and big to survive. Not even Forrester's Landing.

Not really.

Yes they'd saved his life and he would be forever grateful to them but there'd always been a part of him that had felt an outsider. Like he didn't really belong there among the Forrester family that had run the land for generations and the Aboriginal stockmen whose bloodlines and connection with their land ran back another forty thousand years.

Holding Joss felt like...belonging.

"It's been three weeks, Troy." She laughed again, still obviously not taking it seriously. "And you're twenty-seven."

He nodded. "I know. Crazy right?"

"Well...*yes*."

"Look I don't want to make it a...thing. I don't expect anything from you. I know that's not what we're doing here. I don't need reciprocation. I just...I don't know, had to say it."

She blinked. "Oh. *You're serious.*" She tensed. He felt it through her arms and legs and through the tightening of muscles currently cradling his semi-hard cock. "But it's..."

"Crazy?"

"I was going to say absurd."

Troy ignored her dismissive choice of word. "Really, Joss?" he whispered. "Are you that unlovable?"

He kissed her then, slow and gentle, taking his time, loving her mouth as he'd just loved her body—thoroughly. He gave it his all, baring his soul to her. So much of their coming together had been rushed and frantic and he wanted to show her there was more to him than that.

More to them.

More than some wild eight-second ride.

He pulled back, pleased to see the heat glazing her eyes, to hear the catch in her breath. He pushed a wet strand of hair off her shoulders. "I'm pleased I met you, Joss Garrity."

"Oh yeah? Have you forgotten how we met? You *dislo-*

cating your elbow?"

"Have you forgotten we'd already met twice before that?"

She grimaced. "I preferred the third meeting where you were the helpless one for a change."

Troy gave a brief laugh, his gaze roaming over a face that had come to mean so much so quickly. "Something out there sure was determined to get us together."

"Well, for what it's worth, I'm pleased I met you too, Troy Jensen."

Troy's belly squeezed at the admission. It was a start. "Because of all the hot cowboy sex?"

She laughed. "Definitely. But…" She sobered. "For Damien most of all. I feel like I have my son back and a lot of that's because of the example you've set and how good you've been with him. Your assurances that he's going to be okay have meant a lot to me. I owe you for that."

Troy tightened his arms as a sudden jolt of pride and accomplishment shook his chest. It felt better than a gold buckle, a big fat check and a room full of women all dedicated to his pleasure. It felt like he'd come full circle. That he'd finally paid the Forresters' kindness forward.

A thick block of emotion lodged in his throat and pricked at his tear ducts and for a crazy moment he thought he might actually cry. Troy hadn't cried for a very long time and he sure as hell wasn't going to do it now.

He buried his face in her neck and breathed her in, once, twice three times, calming himself. "I have a way you could pay me back?" His voice was muffled but her laugh confirmed she'd heard him clearly enough.

"Oh really?"

He pulled away a little. "Fancy another shower?"

She kissed him, quick and hard. "Yes. But no."

"I promise to do really bad things to you."

Heat shimmered in her gaze for a moment before she said, "Damien…" and wriggled to get down. He eased out of her and slid her to the floor, getting rid of the condom as she picked up the towel and wound it around her body.

She surveyed him as she knotted the towel at her cleavage, her gaze lingering on his junk, which was surprisingly still semi hard despite the fact he'd just had an orgasm that had nearly blown his head off.

"Better make it a cold one," she murmured before stepping out of his reach and sashaying out.

Chapter Fifteen

I THINK I'M falling in love with you, Joss Garrity.

The words still made her swoon hours later. They and what they'd done in the bathroom had played on repeat through Joss's head all afternoon and into the evening as she and Damien waited for Troy's event to begin.

But surprisingly they didn't scare her.

They'd stunned her, of course. They were foolish and impossible and impractical. But they hadn't frightened her. Hadn't forced her into turning tail and running.

She didn't know if it was because she was away from home, from the prying eyes of well-meaning people, from routine and responsibilities, or because she was on his turf but hell if part of her wasn't just a little bit titillated by the idea.

It didn't seem to matter how many times she told herself that his surprise admission was some kind of post-coital endorphin rush, a tiny little squiggle of pleasure wormed its way into her belly every time she thought about it.

She refused to think about it seriously. Refused to let her mind build castles in the sky. Refused to let what he said have an impact on her feelings for him.

She liked Troy. A lot. Period. He was fun and good for Damien and great with Gus and had made her laugh and given her something precious these last few weeks.

But she didn't love him. She *couldn't* love him. It was preposterous. She'd known him for *three* weeks.

True, she'd fallen for Andy very quickly too. Had been smitten at first sight. Had known on their first date that he was really special. Had slept with him on their third. But she'd been *nineteen*. Flights of fancy were fine when you were nineteen.

She was thirty-four. With a dead husband and a teenager and a father-in-law. She had debts and commitments and responsibilities. She was an ER doctor for crying out loud.

ER doctors did not *swoon*.

This wasn't a relationship. It wasn't even the prelude to a relationship. The very idea of it was fanciful. Troy wasn't the kind of guy who tied himself down. And she wasn't looking to tie him down, either.

If Troy got the points he needed here he'd be whisked back into the high-paying, high-stakes extreme circuit. He'd be hitting Tucson in three weeks' time and she'd be a distant memory. She was a roll in the hay to him. A pleasant diversion. She had *no* problems with it. *Really she didn't.*

So why did he have to go and say he thought he was falling in love with her?

And what did that even mean? For her there were no

shades of gray where love was concerned. You were either in it or you weren't. And if you were, you wanted to be a part of that person's life.

Like she had with Andy.

But what did it mean to a twenty-seven-year-old footloose and fancy-free bull rider with the world at his feet?

I love you—it's been fun, bye-bye?

I love you—see you again next year?

I love you—drop everything and live in a gypsy caravan with me?

None of it was practical. Their lifestyles were worlds apart and she wasn't just responsible for herself.

Not that she thought Damien would object to Troy being a bigger part of their lives. He clearly thought Troy walked on water. And he'd been good for Damien. Spending time with him in the long summer evenings after work, talking endlessly about the circuit bulls over which Damien had developed a fixation.

He'd thrown a ball around the backyard with him, showed him how to change a light bulb, replace a fuse and do a grease and oil change on a car.

The kind of stuff a father would do.

The last thing she wanted, though, was to get Damien's hopes up over something that could only ever, practically, be a fling. Joss felt like she was finally getting her son back; she wouldn't jeopardize that by starting something with someone who couldn't give her what she and Damien needed.

Someone who stayed.

If she ever brought a man into their lives, it would be because he was going to be a permanent fixture and Troy was the very definition of temporary.

I think I'm falling in love with you, Joss Garrity.

The thought of it might be doing funny things to her pulse here in this stadium, in Troy's world, waiting to watch him ride but it *wasn't* her world, it wasn't real life and she'd be wise to remember that.

"It should be starting any minute now," Damien said, interrupting her thoughts.

Joss smiled at his transformation as he leaned eagerly forward in his seat. He was wearing a cowboy hat and boots for the love of Mike!

Damien was a city kid, through and through. He'd been scathing about the kids at school who got around in hats and boots and had a running argument with Gus over the country music radio station he insisted on listening to in the car and over breakfast.

And now here he was—thanks to Troy—country to his bootstraps.

Suddenly the lights went low in the stadium and he jumped to his feet with the rest of the crowd, whooping and hollering. "You wait til you see these bulls, Mom," he said as he sat and the announcer boomed introductions into the microphone. "They're terrifying. It's awesome."

Joss smiled. Terrifying wasn't her kind of awesome but

there was no denying Damien was hooked. He'd become a walking encyclopedia on the animals in the last couple of weeks.

He was right—they were terrifying. Troy had got them ringside seats and they were right in the middle of the action. Watching a bull fly out of a chute with a rider on his back on the television did not do the reality any justice.

The first two bull riders landed on their butts in under four seconds. Joss hadn't been able to watch the bone-jarring impact.

"Please tell me you don't want to do that," she said as they waited for the third cowboy to come out of the chute.

"Hell no, I'd rather get through life without any broken bones."

Joss breathed a sigh of relief. Whatever else Damien had become these last few years he was still the son of a doctor.

"I want to be a stock contractor."

Joss blinked at the definitive statement. "Oh." Damien had already talked incessantly about Troy's friend Rowan but she hadn't realized he was *that* serious.

"Troy said he could put a good word in for me with Ro's father. He thinks he might take me on after I finish high school, so I could learn the business."

Oh he did, did he? Troy seriously should know better than to plant such possibilities in the head of an impressionable fifteen-year-old without at least talking to her about it first.

"Are you mad I don't want to go to college?"

"No." She was a little ticked at Troy but not Damien. In a perfect world she'd want her son to go to college and get a degree but Andy's death had taught her the world wasn't perfect and life was short. "I want you to be happy, Damien. I want you to do whatever it is you want to do."

"Do you think…Dad would be disappointed if I didn't become an architect?"

"No. Absolutely not." Joss's heart contracted at the sudden streak of uncertainty in her son's voice. Damien had wanted to be an architect like his father for years and had become more adamant about it since his death.

It was moments like these when she realized how deep Damien's grief still ran.

"Your dad understood all about not following family traditions. Your grandfather was none too pleased when he didn't follow him into the fencing business." She squeezed his hand. "He'd want you to do what *you* wanted to do. And he'd have been proud of you no matter what. He was your biggest fan. So am I."

Damien pulled her into a big bear hug. "You're the best, Mom," he whispered and Joss blinked back tears.

The third bull rider fired out of the chute at that moment and Damien's attention snapped back to the arena, gasping at the size of the bull called Skeletor. Joss gasped at something else entirely.

This cowboy wasn't wearing the impressive helmet the

previous two had worn with its jaw protection and facial grill. Just his flimsy felt cowboy hat.

What. The. Hell. *Was he mad?*

Surely there was some kind of law or industry standard that made helmets compulsory? "He's not wearing a helmet," she said to a cheering Damien.

"They don't have to."

Joss gaped. *What?* She couldn't even begin to wrap her head around such stupidity. What was wrong with these people?

At six seconds the guy riding the bull was bucked off. The whole crowd gasped as his glove got stuck in the rope and he was dragged around by the angry, kicking beast. Joss couldn't bear to watch but she couldn't look away either as the rider was finally tossed aside, smacking his head on the ground and landing in a heap.

His stupid useless hat landed near his foot.

Everyone rose, including Joss whose stomach churned at the sickening sight. Her first reaction was to get to him. An instinctual medical response bred into her over years on the job and she hadn't realized she'd turned to do just that until Damien grabbed her arm.

"It's okay, Mom, they have a sports medicine team. See?"

She turned to find three guys running onto the arena with vests emblazoned with *Medical* in fluorescent printing. The bull was still there but being expertly herded by the rodeo clowns toward the open gate.

Joss thought she recognized one of them as he kneeled to the unmoving man and realized he'd come in the ambulance with Troy a few weeks ago.

There was a collective sigh as the cowboy on the ground started to move. Most of the crowd sat but there were a lot of hands pressed to mouths and thundering silence as everyone watched the unfolding drama.

"He'll be all right, Mom," Damien assured her. "Look, see, they're getting him on his feet."

But Joss wasn't so sure. He was very unsteady, clearly dazed. They should have a collar on him; they should have stretchered him off. He staggered and her heart leapt into her mouth as two guys supported him out of the arena.

At best he was concussed. At worst his brain could be actively bleeding.

All because the idiot hadn't been wearing a helmet.

Joss was still trying to grapple with it all when the next cowboy was announced. Apparently nothing stopped because some idiot could be having a cranial hemorrhage.

The show went on.

TROY WAS THE tenth rider in tonight's lineup, which meant Joss had to sit through a lot of guys voluntarily signing up to be tossed in the air and landing in bone-crunching fashion.

Some were luckier than others. Two even landed on their

feet. And two lasted the full eight seconds. None thankfully sustained any injuries and at least they were all wearing helmets.

Still, all the time her mind worried about the injured cowboy.

Then the guy with the mic was announcing Troy and Joss's pulse spiked, her hands curling into fists. She might have thought this was batshit crazy but she knew how much this meant to him.

She was sick to the stomach thinking that he'd land on his arm again and reinjure it.

Please don't get hurt. Please don't get hurt.

"Oh no, he's drawn Excalibur," Damien said, almost as tense as she was.

Joss glanced at her son. "Is that bad?"

"He's one of the meanest bulls on the pro circuit."

"God," she wailed. *Please don't get hurt.* "Don't tell me that."

Damien took her hand. "He just has to go eight seconds."

The chute opened then with a bang, startling Joss, and Troy was flung out on the back of Excalibur. She leapt to her feet with Damien. He was going nuts but Joss was dumbstruck, too shocked to say anything.

He wasn't wearing a helmet.

His long lanky body was being pitched to and fro and side to side like a rag doll with absolutely no protection for his head at all.

Just that stupid cowboy hat.

Her heart was beating so hard she thought it was going to crack a rib and she was so close to losing the hotdog she'd eaten she swallowed hard.

"He's not wearing a helmet."

She thought she'd said it to herself but she must have said it loud enough for Damien to hear it over the crowd.

"He'll be fine, Mom," he yelled.

The buzzer rang out and the crowd went nuts, the announcer waxing lyrical about Troy being on fire and clawing back his place in the extreme comp. Damien turned and hugged her, actually lifting her off her feet for a second or two before letting her down. "He did, Mom! He did it."

She watched in a numb kind of daze as he was pitched off the back of the bull, landing on the ground on his side but springing immediately to his feet and moving in the opposite direction to the bull as the clowns distracted Excalibur.

He picked up his stupid hat and waved it at the crowd, seeking them out among the cheering masses, giving them the thumbs-up with a big grin before running out of the arena.

Damien whooped as he sat down. "That was *awesome!*"

Joss shook her head. She felt sick. That anyone would so blatantly pay so little heed to the dangers of bull riding was incomprehensible but Troy…?

What the hell was she doing with him?

With someone who had so little respect for his own life? She knew what he did was dangerous but she'd have thought he'd at least take every precaution to minimize harm. He wore a protective vest but not anything to keep his head from being crushed?

Andy hadn't been able to control the freak accident that had killed him but if he could have, he would have. He would have done *anything, given* anything to be around to see his son grow up, to grow old with her.

And here was Troy, with a complete disregard for his life, dicing with death every weekend.

Anger churned in her gut. She couldn't watch another moment. *She had to get out.*

"Come on." She stood. "Let's go."

Damien glanced at her, startled. "*What?*"

"I've seen enough. We're leaving."

He frowned. "It's not over yet, Mom. There's more in this round and Troy's advanced to the second round."

"I don't care." Anger was turning to rage. Her hands were actually shaking.

"What's wrong?" he demanded.

"Nothing. We're just done here."

She was *so* done here.

But of course, Damien wasn't. He shook his head, his jaw jutting out. "I'm not. And I'm not leaving." That bullish expression she was used to made an appearance. "We're

Troy's guests; we can't just leave. You're the one who taught me that."

If her son thought he could guilt her into staying then he was dead wrong. "Oh yes we can."

"I don't *want* to."

The announcer was introducing the next rider and Joss didn't know how much longer she'd be able to keep her stomach contents down. Short of physically dragging him out, there wasn't much she could do and she didn't want to cause a public spectacle.

But she was damned if she was sticking around.

"Fine." Troy had shown them where to meet him after the show. Damien was old enough to be left unsupervised and he had a phone. "I'll text Troy and let him know I've left and he's to bring you to straight back to the motel after."

Damien nodded, his features softening now he had his own way. "Are you okay, Mom?"

"I'm fine," she assured him.

Or she would be anyway.

JOSS WAS PACING when she heard the lock whir just after eleven. She'd already packed their bags and stowed them in the car.

Thank God they'd brought two.

She whirled to face the door to find an ecstatic Damien

chattering away, obviously unconcerned about her earlier mood. Troy was more subdued, eyeing her warily over Damien's head. He was in jeans and a checked shirt, the sleeves rolled up, his hat crammed on his head, looking every inch the cocky young cowboy who'd pulled over to help her with her tire a few weeks ago.

Which only made her madder.

He glanced around the room and she clocked the moment he realized the absence of *stuff*. No more of Damien's clothes spread over his bed. The cupboards where she'd stowed her bag and hung a couple of shirts, empty.

"Mom!" Damien threw an arm around Troy's shoulder. "He did it! Two eight-second rides!"

Joss smiled stiffly. Unfortunately time and distance had not helped the situation. Neither had the last two hours Googling bull rider injuries. "Congratulations."

Her red-hot rage from earlier had crystallized to a deep icy anger.

Damien prattled on about the second ride she'd missed as he headed to his bed ignorant of her cool formality. "Where's my stuff?" He looked around.

"It's in the car. We're leaving. Would you mind waiting for me there, please? I'll only be a few minutes."

"*What?*"

"I said we're leaving. Get in the car."

Damien glanced at Troy as if he had some kind of answer. Troy, who was standing with his hands in his back pockets, shrugged. Damien looked at Joss. "What the hell's going on?"

"Nothing. Something…came up. That's all."

Damien's brown eyes crinkled as he took a step toward her. "Is Grandpa okay?"

Joss's heart swelled in her chest at his immediate concern considering how pissed off he clearly was. "No, he's fine. I'll explain in the car."

Somehow…

He crossed his arms. "But we've still got another night."

"Damien…*please*." For the love of Mike would he just do something she asked for once! "I'm not going to argue with you about this."

He opened his mouth to do just that but Troy cut him off. "It's okay, mate." He gave Damien a reassuring smile. "Just do as your mom asks, okay?"

"But it's stupid!"

One side of Troy's mouth kicked up. "Sometimes you gotta do things for people you love." He glanced at her. "Even when they're stupid."

Damien glared mutinously from one to the other before he stomped out of the room and slammed the door behind him for good measure.

"Okay." Troy took off his hat and threw it on the closest bed. "You going to tell me what happened tonight?"

Chapter Sixteen

JOSS QUIRKED AN eyebrow. "How's the guy who landed on his head?"

He frowned. "Renaldo? His scans are clear. He's staying in overnight to monitor his concussion. He'll probably be back competing tomorrow night."

"*What?*" The ice in her chest exploded in a flash of heat.

He shrugged like concussion was the equivalent to a hangnail. "Can't keep a good rider down."

"That's the stupidest thing I've ever heard," she snapped. "The rodeo sports medicine people will just *let* him do that?"

"Well they'll put him through some tests first but yeah…if he passes…"

Joss was temporarily speechless. Even in football they wouldn't let a concussed man get back on the field so soon after sustaining his injury.

"Why don't you wear a helmet?"

"Ah." She saw the light dawn then. "*That's* what this is about?"

His incredulity spiked her blood pressure. "Yes. That. The trivial matter of your stupid head being stomped on by a one-ton bull or cracking it so hard against the ground your brain starts to bleed and swell and if it doesn't kill you will probably leave you a vegetable for the rest of your life."

"Whoa there." Troy laughed. "I see what Damien means about the medical horror stories."

His laugh was like a red rag to the proverbial bull. "How can you trivialize this?" She stalked toward him, covering the distance between them, stopping just short of being able to push him in the chest. "It's your head!" she yelled.

"Okay, wait, stop." He held up his hands. "I'm sorry, I didn't mean to trivialize anything.

"*Why?* Why don't you wear a helmet?"

"Because a hat looks cooler."

Joss gaped at him. "You're shitting me, right?"

"I want to look like a bloody cowboy, not a damn hockey player."

Joss moved away abruptly in case she gave in to the temptation to smack some sense into him. She twirled to face him once she was a safe distance. "You really are just a bloody big overgrown *boy* aren't you? That's something I'd expect Damien to say!"

She didn't need two teenage boys in her life.

"You wear a vest? Why not a helmet?"

"I have to wear a vest, Joss. It's the rules."

"Others wear helmets."

He nodded. "It's a personal choice. Not one I that I've made for me."

"What if I asked you to make it for me?" Joss knew she had no right to ask, no real claim on him but she couldn't bear the thought of him going in to that ring again in his cowboy hat.

He looked taken aback for a moment. "I…"

Joss felt his hesitation right down to her marrow. Of course. Why would he make such a choice for some woman he'd spent a few weeks with?

"I'll be all right you know. Really."

"How?" The question exploded from her lips, her heart beating hard. "How do you know that? I've spent the last two hours Googling bull-riding injuries and no one can say that as a certainty."

He grimaced. "You probably shouldn't have done that."

"Ya think?"

"Look." He took a step toward her. She took a step back and he halted before taking his next step, shoving his hands on his hips. "I survive on my instincts out there. On my gut. I know how to land. How to protect my head."

Joss couldn't stop the hysterical bubble of laughter. "I can't do this, Troy. I can't go out there and watch you be so irresponsible with your life." To her surprise a tear trekked down her cheek and she dashed it away, pissed off by its very presence. "Don't come back home after tomorrow. *Please.* It's going to be hard enough for Damien to separate from you. Best make a clean break."

"*Joss.*"

He covered the distance between them ignoring her hand signal to stop, pulling up in front of her, a handbreadth away. Joss could barely breathe, a wild tangle of emotions clogging her chest.

"Please don't do this. You do get immune to the dangers pretty quickly, I promise."

Joss gave a half laugh. "I don't *want* to get immune to them. *Nobody* should be immune to them. This is serious stuff, Troy."

She searched his face for recognition. For a sign that he knew how important his damn head was. But all she saw was a young guy who thought he was bulletproof.

"Look…it's been a fun pit stop for you. And for me. But it's over."

He slipped his hands onto her elbows. "That's not what this has been. I meant what I said before. I'm in love with you, Joss. Give me a chance."

In love with. No *think I might be* this time. God…she'd known him for three weeks but already a cramp was flaring behind her sternum.

"Jesus, Troy…" She pulled her arms away and moved back a step. "I don't need a cocky young cowboy with a death wish in my life and I definitely *don't* need another man in my *son's* life who's going to not come home one day."

"I'm careful, Joss. Really careful."

"No." She shook her head. "My husband…he was careful. He worked in an office and we bought in a safe neighborhood. He always got the car serviced on time and was pedantic about shoveling the snow from the path every winter so we wouldn't break our necks. And looked what happened to him."

Joss smashed her right fist into her left palm. The noise was loud in the silent room and she swore she saw Troy flinch a little.

"Boom! Car totaled. Dead. Gone." She snapped her fingers. "Just like that. Andy would have given *anything* to still be alive and kicking today. To be around, watching his son grow up and here *you* are—" She poked him hard in the chest. "Deliberating, willfully, *recklessly* endangering your life. Every weekend."

"Exactly. I could give it up tomorrow and there'd be absolutely no guarantee that something terrible won't happen to me just walking down the street."

"I'm not asking you to give it up, Troy, certainly not for me. I'm asking you to be *smart*. I know there aren't any guarantees in life."

"Joss…" He shoved a hand over his head. "What I do is actually a helluva lot safer than driving. I'm statistically much more likely to die in a car accident than I am being killed by a bull."

"Yeah, but people who drive cars do everything they can to keep safe. They put on their seat belts and manufacturers make cars with airbags, reversing cameras and advanced braking systems. You know…" Joss shook her head. "I look after people who are clinging to life with their *fingernails*, who'd give anything for another day and you just…"

She waved her hand dismissively, her feelings too tangled to articulate.

"You're a doctor," he said gently. "You have a skewed view of things. It's taught you to see the dangers in everything."

"You know what medicine has taught me? That life is precious and is a helluva lot more preferable than being dead." She supposed absently that Troy hadn't come from a background where any of that had been reinforced. "And you should be doing everything you can to stay alive because you're worth it."

Had his upbringing caused such a disregard for his own life? Was he still, deep down, that abused child who didn't think himself worthy of life?

He opened his mouth to say something but the door suddenly opened and a thunderous-looking Damien glared at her.

"Are we going or not?"

Joss nodded, grateful for the reprieve, her heart unbearably heavy. There was no point staying and going around and around the houses with Troy.

"I'm coming."

The door slammed shut again and she stepped around Troy, ignoring the brush of his hand as he reached out to touch her on the way past.

"I love you."

Her step faltered but she didn't stop. She didn't answer. She just kept going. All the way out the door and to her car. She'd known him for three lousy weeks and he had a death wish.

She *did not* love him.

She would not.

TROY WON THE next night. He scored some cash and enough points to get back into the extreme tour but the victory was a brittle one.

He should have been ecstatic. Prior to Plainview, he would have partied hard. Booze and women for sure. But it suddenly didn't appeal. He wanted Joss. To celebrate with *her*. And Damien.

He wanted to go *home*.

He hadn't realized until now that a *pers*on could be home.

The places he'd grown up in had been dives and hovels. Four walls barely containing the dysfunction within. No love. No connection.

But he knew now deep in his soul that *Joss* was his home.

He didn't turn his pickup in her direction, though. Not yet. *He wasn't giving up.* He just figured that maybe she needed some time to cool down. Some time to miss him.

And he needed to get his head in the game. He'd been seriously mentally AWOL these last few weeks and that wasn't how you won comps.

Tucson was in three weeks and he needed a big comeback. *He needed to win.* And not just for the money or the points. He needed to prove to them all—cowboys, sponsors, fans—that he may have been down but he wasn't out.

That the Wonder from Down Under was back. And he was playing to win.

After Tucson he'd try again. Try to make her understand that he knew what he was doing. That the iconic image of a cowboy on the back of a bull, his hand held high, his hat firmly in place, was a powerful brand.

The kind sponsors and fans went nuts for.

And if she wouldn't listen then he'd just keep going back and back and wearing her down little by little. He knew she felt something for him too—why worry about his head if she didn't care about him?

Because she was a doctor? He didn't buy that.

So he needed to maintain a presence in her life. Turning up between rodeos when the schedule allowed. Showing her he was serious about a relationship with her. Chipping away at her concerns.

But his plan for now was to give her some space.

He pushed on to Roswell with the pro circuit. He'd always liked New Mexico. So much of the topography reminded him of the Top End. He'd been to Santa Fe multiple times over the years, the last time in April as part of the extreme circuit—he'd come third.

Plus it was close to Tucson. Close to Joss.

He was surprised to stumble across one of the ranked cowboys from the extreme circuit at the start of the second night in Roswell. T.J. Casey was one tough mother of a cowboy, currently ranked fourth overall and Troy's competition. But by and large, they all got along out of the arena.

"Hey, dude," Troy said as they slapped each other on the back. "I heard you were missing Sacramento."

"Yeah." The other man grimaced, his hand gripping his left shoulder. "Gave it a bit of a nudge. I'll be good for San Diego though."

"Whatcha doing down this way?"

"Heard about this rookie on the pro circuit. Thought I'd come and check him out."

"Diego? Yeah, he's gonna be big, man. He's been on my ass at every event. I swear that kid was born with bum glue."

Casey laughed and they headed into the arena together to watch the show. Afterward they found the bar at Troy's hotel.

It wasn't really Troy's scene. He preferred bare boards underfoot and country music on the juke box. This was more like an airport lounge with elevator music but they served booze and it was near deserted, which meant nobody was going to be hassling them for autographs.

Casey ordered a beer but Troy needed something stronger. His nights had been restless, filled with images of Joss and the things they'd done together and wiping himself out on hard liquor was the only thing that got him through the cravings.

"Tequila. Straight up."

Casey, who'd ordered a beer, cocked an eyebrow as the bartender poured a shot glass in front of them. "Going straight for the hard stuff? Must be a woman."

Troy ignored him, tapped his glass on the bar and tossed it back. It burned all the way down, licking tongues of fire along his nerve endings. He placed the empty in front of him and said, "Another."

"Definitely a woman. C'mon, man, out with it. You can tell your Uncle Casey anything. You know I don't gossip."

Troy downed the second shot. "Another."

Casey whistled. "Man…she's got you real worked up." He eyed Troy as he threw back his third shot. "What's her name?"

Troy *thunked* the glass on the glossy wooden surface. The barman lifted the tequila bottle in silent question and Troy nodded but he didn't touch the shot after it was poured. His tongue felt numb and he was feeling sufficiently lubed to open up.

"Joss." Hell, he missed saying her name.

Casey laughed. "Hey, can you hear that? The sound of a thousand buckle bunny hearts breaking all over the land." He clapped Troy on the back. "Can't wait to tell the guys

The Wonder from Down Under has got himself all hung up over a woman."

Troy grunted. "Don't get too carried away. I'm not exactly her favorite person, you know?"

"Aw, hell, man. You screwed up?"

"What in hell makes you think *I* screwed up?"

"C'mon. I've known you for a few years. You're great with onetime deals but you don't do anything more serious."

"For fuck's sake, all I did was tell her I love her."

"*You* said the L word?"

Casey laughed like that was the funniest thing he'd ever heard. Troy stared into his drink, waiting for him to stop.

"No offense, man, but you got so many notches on your belt I didn't think you even knew what that was."

"Well I do. Now. When you've never been in love before, it's pretty fucking obvious." For someone who'd lived his entire life with an absence of love, it was blindingly evident when it did happen.

This thing he felt for Joss was totally alien to him. He'd been with a lot of women—none of them had ever made him feel the way he felt about Joss.

"In my admittedly not in-depth experience with women, they tend to like it when you say the L word so what else did you do?"

"She's pissed at me over not wearing a helmet. She's an ER doc and a widow. Husband died in a car crash. She's got a fifteen-year-old kid." He shrugged. "She thinks I have some kind of reckless death wish."

"So?" Casey shrugged. "Wear the damn helmet."

"And hide this pretty face?" Troy absently twisted his full shot glass on the bar surface. "They're ugly-ass things."

Casey huffed out a sympathetic laugh. "Maybe. But she's right—they're safer. And you know sooner or later, they'll be compulsory anyway."

Troy nodded. The writing had been on the wall for a while.

"You ever thought about what you're going to do after all this?" Casey asked. "When you're too busted up to get on the back of a bull?"

Troy shook his head. "Nope. I'm not like you. I didn't come into this with an exit strategy. To be honest, I always kind of figured that I'd get stomped by some ornery bull and it'd be all over."

He'd figured it wouldn't be such a bad way to die. Quick. Doing something he loved. Going down in a blaze of glory.

"Man." Casey frowned over top of his beer. "That's pretty fucked up."

"Yeah." He clinked his shot glass against Casey's bottle and knocked the tequila back.

Casey's gaze was heavy on his profile. "Maybe you *should* start thinking about an exit strategy?"

Troy watched the barman pour more clear liquid into his glass. Maybe he should. Because now there was Joss. And

Damien.

And love.

CASEY'S WORDS PLAYED on Troy's mind as he meandered around New Mexico. He didn't have any particular destination in mind, just driving from town to town, playing tourist, stopping at roadside motels for the night, drinking too much then moseying off the next day to a new place.

There was a restlessness he couldn't ignore, though.

Troy had spent seven years in the US, doing just this. Driving around the country, going from event to event. Sometimes with other cowboys for company, but mostly by himself.

And he'd loved it.

The big open spaces had called to him, filled him up. He'd felt comfortable being alone with the grandeur of nature. Probably in some kind of deeply fucked-up way, the immensity of nature confirmed what he'd been told his whole life by his parents.

He was small, he was no one, he was insignificant. And that's why he felt so comfortable alone in it.

But it was different now. Now there was Joss and he wanted to be *significant*. To her. And Damien. He certainly didn't want to be alone anymore. He had no doubt he could hook up every night with a different woman until he left this earth but he'd been doing that for the last seven years and not one of them had made him feel any less alone.

Not like Joss. Just thinking about her filled up his head and his heart. He could see a whole future with her. A whole new world.

For the first time ever he was thinking beyond the next rodeo thanks to Casey's question needling him every moment of the day.

The last place he expected to find the answer was in New Mexico.

He'd set out for Tucson on the Monday before the extreme event. Figured he'd take a couple of days to get there then kick around the city for a bit. But then he passed a *For Sale* sign on a ranch near Artesia and, for some reason he couldn't explain, stopped to check it out.

The twelve thousand acre ranch hadn't been occupied for a while. It was run-down and needed work. But it had everything required for a working cattle ranch as well as a sprawling, Spanish-style homestead, perfect for a family.

An idea crystallized in his bones—so strong and clear it couldn't be ignored. He contacted the realtor immediately and after a couple of days of lawyers and accountants and high finance, he laid down a cool two mill and bought it.

A lot of the cowboys on the extreme circuit owned working cattle ranches but Troy's was going to be different. It was time to pay things forward. To offer kids like he'd been a chance at redemption. The kind of chance that came with hard work and grit and someone willing to give them a second chance. Like the Forresters had done for him.

He was going to establish a dude ranch. For delinquents.

Troy had *no* idea how to go about establishing it but that didn't matter because he'd work it out. For the first time in his life he was dreaming of a future. There was only one thing missing.

And it was time to go get her.

Chapter Seventeen

Troy pulled up outside Joss's house at eight on Wednesday night. Gus answered the door. "Hello, son." He held out his hand and Troy shook it.

"Is Joss home?" If she was at work he'd just go to the hospital.

"She is." Gus regarded him for long moments, his arm slung casually across the doorway. "You have feelings for her, son?"

"Yes, sir, I do." He hadn't called Gus sir since that first day but if there was a moment for it, this was it. His mouth dried with a sudden attack of nerves. "I know Andy was your son, and I'm sorry if that's hard for you to hear. I don't want to take his place in Joss or Damien's life. But I do want to be part of theirs. If she'll have me."

Gus nodded slowly. "Andy wouldn't have wanted Joss to be alone forever. He'd have wanted her to love again. And I think he would have liked you, son. But you break her heart and I will kick your ass. I may be seventy but I can still lay it down, you hear?"

Troy smiled grudgingly. "Yes, sir."

He stood aside. "Come on in."

Troy shook his head. "If you don't mind, I'll stay right here. Save her having to kick me out if she doesn't like what I have to say."

He needed *her* to invite him into her life. And that started at her front door.

Gus nodded. "I'll go get her. I think she's out back."

Time dragged by and the knot of nerves in his stomach screwed tighter until he could almost feel the lump beneath his skin. For an awful moment Troy entertained the possibility she might refuse to see him.

Then what would he do?

Walk around the damn back, that's what. He wasn't leaving here without talking to her tonight.

But finally she came to the door, that short cotton gown pulled tight beneath her folded arms, wrapped around her like armor. Her hair was pulled back into its regulation swishy ponytail. Her feet were bare.

Troy's chest tightened at the sight of her and he shoved his hands into his back pockets to stop himself from yanking her into his arms.

"Hi."

She didn't really look at him directly and barely acknowledged his greeting before saying, "What do you want, Troy?"

He took a steadying breath. "I'm going to wear the helmet. In Tucson. And from now on."

If she was relieved she didn't let on. She didn't sag or relax her posture. "Because of me?"

"Yes."

"I'd rather you wore it because of you." Her voice was snippy as her fingers squeezed and released her biceps.

"I'm wearing the damn helmet, Joss." Troy kept his temper in check. "If you want me to like wearing it as well that's going to take a bit longer."

She glared at him. Now he had her full attention. "It's not about the *damn* helmet."

He cocked an eyebrow. "Excuse me?"

"Okay, well maybe it is about the helmet a little." She sighed and relaxed slightly, leaning her shoulder into the doorframe. "I've had time to think about it, Troy... I just don't see how you and I will work."

And here he was thinking giving her time would work in his favor.

"We have different lifestyles. You follow the circuit around for most of the year and I'm entrenched in this community. I can't drop everything and go on the road with you. I have a kid and a job I love. And long-distance relationships are hard. Not a lot of them work out. You'll grow tired of this and one night there'll be some party somewhere and some pretty young available thing—"

"No!" Troy interrupted her with a vehement headshake. "Absolutely not."

"It's okay, I wouldn't blame you for it. You're twenty-seven and women throw themselves at you. That's a *lot* of temptation for any guy."

Troy's jaw almost cracked he was clenching it so hard. "You think I can't keep my cock in my pants?" he demanded, his voice low but flinty.

She had the good grace to blush but she didn't back down either. "I think you've never *had* to. That might be a harder habit to break than you realize."

Troy shoved a hand through his hair. "I would never cheat on you. *Never.* Jesus, Joss, I love you."

"Troy…" She looked at him with actual pity this time. "Please stop with the love stuff… We barely know each other."

He lost the battle with trying to keep his temper in check. "I know you think it's too quick and that I'm too young for you. What would I know about love, right?" He shook his head, her pity and doubt cut deep. "Well I can tell you, as someone who's had absolutely *no* experience with love in his life *whatsoever,* when it happens, you recognize it, like that."

Troy snapped his fingers. He'd told her he thought he was falling in love with her in Lubbock but the truth was he'd fallen for her that night with the lug wrench. "They say a man can't miss what he doesn't know but that's bullshit. I never knew what love felt like. Not until you, Joss. And it's like a knife in my gut to think I've missed out on that all my life."

Her eyes filled with tears. "Oh Troy—"

"No," he interrupted. "Just wait." He didn't want her pity. "I have more to say. You told me I had a death wish and I guess you were right. I never really much cared whether I lived or died. I think that's why bull riding appealed. Seemed like a surefire way to go and that was okay because there was no one around who'd mourn me. Nobody I'd really miss either. My exit plan from the circuit was a coffin. But that was before you."

A tear slipped down her face and she wiped it away. "What you do is so dangerous," she murmured. "I can't bury another man. It would kill me the second time around."

Troy finally understood that this was the real crux of the issue with Joss. Not his age or how quickly it had all moved. She'd lost someone she cared for deeply already. "I know. That's why I have a better exit plan now."

She looked at him sharply and even though her eyes were two gray puddles he could see *hope* in them.

"I just bought a ranch. In New Mexico. It's not far from Artesia. I want to turn it into a working cattle ranch where troubled youth can come for a second chance, get their lives together. Like what the Forresters did for me but on a more formal scale. We could breed bulls for the rodeo circuit if Damien's still serious about getting into stock contracting and there's a hospital thirty miles away."

She blinked, clearly surprised. "You...want us to move to New Mexico with you?"

Troy nodded. "I do. It's not that far and if you're worried about Gus, don't be. I hope he comes too. The house is big enough for all of us and I could do with another handy guy around. The fences are shit, they all need redoing and I bet there's plenty of work in the area."

"So…" She frowned. "You're giving up the circuit?"

The note of hope in her voice was barely constrained and he wanted to be able to tell her yes but he couldn't. "Not straight away. I want to finish the year, try to grab the big prize money in Forth Worth." God knew he was probably going to need it given the chunk he'd just taken out of his savings.

"Oh. I see."

"I know long-distance relationships are hard but it's only two months and I will spend as much time back here with you in between events. If…" Troy held his breath "…you'll have me."

"Troy…" She shook her head as if to clear it. "This is…a lot to take in. Six weeks ago I didn't even know you and now you want me to pick up my kid and my father-in-law and…move to another state, another house, another job?"

She was looking at him like he'd lost his mind but she was wrong. Troy was finally in his *right* mind. "Forget that for a moment." He waved a dismissive hand. "How do you *feel* about me, Joss?

Her gaze met his. "I don't know," she whispered. "This whole thing is…crazy."

Troy's chest cramped. It wasn't what he'd hoped to hear but she was chewing on her bottom lip, looking somewhere between doubtful and terrified and that was on him. He'd gone too far, too fast and overwhelmed her.

He *was* asking a lot of her. No matter how much it killed him, he had to slow it down.

"You're right, I'm sorry. I'm rushing you and I don't want you to make any hasty decision."

Especially a hasty no.

"Don't give me an answer tonight. I'm going to get in my pickup now and head to Tucson and while I'm winning that sucker you can have some time and space to think about things. And then I'll come back next week and we can talk. Okay?"

She nodded. "Okay." But Troy wasn't sure she'd taken it all in. She was clearly flummoxed and already grappling with the things he'd said.

He stepped in then and kissed her. Light and gentle. A brief press of his mouth to hers but it still took all his willpower to pull away. "I'll see you next week."

Before he had a chance to turn away she said, "Thank you. For wearing the helmet."

Troy smiled and touched the rim of his hat in a small salute. Then turned and walked to his pickup.

Gus put a plate of bacon and eggs in front of Joss on Sunday morning. She wasn't hungry. She hadn't been hungry all week but she picked up her utensils, feigning interest. He sat and handed her an envelope.

Joss frowned. "What's this?"

Gus exchanged a glance with Damien. Whatever it was they were in cahoots. "It's a gift."

Joss opened the envelope warily to find a return airline ticket. To Tucson. For two this afternoon. And a ticket to the Extreme Bull Riders event. Thanks to Damien, she already knew Troy had reached the championship round.

Her heart skipped a beat as she glanced sharply at the two men in her life. "Gus…I can't." She pushed the envelope across the table.

She'd been going over and over what Troy had said since he left. And she kept circling back around to having known him for such a short time.

"Are you worried about Dad, Mom?" Damien was looking at her so earnestly, so grown up, Joss wanted to cry. "Because you told me he'd want me to be whatever I wanted to be. And I might have only been ten when he passed but I remember him too, Mom. And *I* know he'd want you to be happy."

"The boy's right."

Joss cleared her throat of the sudden burr of emotion. "I'm happy."

Both of them looked at her in disbelief. "You've been

distracted and irritable since you came back from Lubbock like a bat out of hell that night." Gus was his usual straight-talking self. "You're obviously not sleeping if those bags under your eyes are anything to go on and you've been moping around the house since he left on Wednesday. What did he want?"

Joss hadn't been aware of her behavior. Or the bags. She thought she'd been going out of her way to project normality. Obviously not well enough. Or maybe Gus was just practiced at seeing through her veneer after Andy.

Either way, it wasn't fair on either of them to have to tiptoe around her.

"He's bought a ranch in New Mexico and he wants us all to go and live with him there. He wants to breed bulls, help Damien get into the contracting business and be a place where troubled kids can get a chance to turn their lives around."

Damien's face lit up. "For real?"

"For real."

"And how do you feel about that?" Gus pressed.

She shook her head. "I've known him for *six* weeks."

"And how long did you know Andy before you knew how you felt about him?"

Joss shoved her elbows on the table and rubbed her temples, eyes fixed on the tabletop. "A month."

"Exactly." Gus nodded.

"I was *nineteen*, Gus."

"Do you think being stupid in love depends how old you are? You think love gives a crap about age?"

Damien laughed because his grandfather didn't often use bad language. And old people cussing was universally hilarious to fifteen-year-olds.

"Joss..." His voice was quiet yet somehow still compelled her to look at him. "Life's short. *You* know that better than anybody. You're still young and he loves you, right?"

Joss's face warmed. Having this conversation in front of her son wasn't ideal but Damien was as interested in the answer as Gus. "He says so."

"And you love him?"

Joss opened her mouth to refute it or to obfuscate but something let go in her chest at that moment. She'd been denying the truth for weeks now but it suddenly ruptured in her chest like a blown vessel.

God help her she did. She *did* love him.

It wasn't practical or wise. But it was there. New and glowing and insistent. Like it had been in the beginning with Andy complete with hammering heart and the mad, crushing desire to be with him.

"Yes."

Gus nodded. "Then the rest can be worked out." He pushed the envelope back across the table. "Go get your man, Joss."

Pressure built in her chest and she felt short of breath as her nose prickled with threatening tears.

Why did love always feel like a heart attack?

"Better put on some makeup though." Damien grinned. "Those bags are bad."

Joss laughed despite the ache in her chest. She reached her hand across the table and Damien interlinked his fingers with hers.

"Go get him, Mom."

EVERYTHING CONSPIRED AGAINST Joss. Road works on the way to Lubbock, the nearest airport, made the trip longer and then the plane was delayed half an hour due to some issues on the ground. Thankfully changing flights at Phoenix went smoothly but they were put in a holding pattern over Tucson due to storms. By the time she got to the venue the show had already started.

The Joss from six weeks ago would have taken that as *a sign*. The newly in love Joss wasn't letting anything stop her from getting her man.

The stadium was much bigger than the one in Lubbock. And it was packed to the gills. She could barely hear herself think as she finally took her seat. Which was just as well—she was a bundle of nerves now.

Both for Troy and for her.

This was a big night for him—his return to the extreme circuit. He'd pinned his hopes on winning and she wanted him to win just as badly. Even if she had to watch his ass being tossed off a bull over and over.

But at least he was wearing a helmet. It was obviously a big enough thing for the announcer to make a mention of it and for the people surrounding her to talk about it too.

Mostly not favorable.

Apparently they'd rather see his sexy face than worry about the brain behind it.

Joss didn't care. Her heart swelled with pride and with love and when he went eight seconds, she was on her feet with everyone else.

Troy rode like he was born on a bull, making two more eight-second rides, on the meanest bulls Joss had seen, going down to the wire with a guy called Casey who was ranked number four. At the end of the night everything rode on the points for his final ride on a big black bull called Road to Ruin.

When he scored an eighty-eight, putting him one point ahead of Casey, the whole stadium went nuts for the underdog who'd been busted down to the pro circuit and won on his comeback event.

So did Joss. She was laughing and crying and hugging complete strangers all around her, even the ones who cared more about Troy's face than his brain. It had been a nerve-racking, exhilarating, emotionally exhausting evening and there was more where that came from.

The night wasn't over yet.

Joss has no idea where the cowboys dressing area was but a group of giggling women passed her talking about getting autographs and she followed them. The women stopped with a small crowd of other people around the back of the stadium just short of a couple of security guards. A door was open behind them and she could see the occasional flash of fringed chaps.

Joss wasn't prepared to hang back. She'd come this far; she didn't want to wait around any longer. She approached one of the security guards. "Hey," she said, smiling big and friendly. "I'm after Troy. Jensen."

He gave her a quick once-over and obviously didn't think she was Troy's *type*. So much for her effort with the makeup. He gave her a tight smile. "I'm sorry, ma'am, we can't let anyone through."

Not to be deterred, Joss changed tack. "He's expecting me."

Another doubtful look. "I'm sorry, ma'am. Mr. Jensen has given specific orders that no women are to be admitted to see him."

Joss grinned stupidly at the security guard who probably thought she was not only fooling herself but was slightly unhinged as well. Troy had *specifically asked* no women to be admitted.

She almost happy danced.

"I'll text him," she said, still smiling despite being thwarted. "You'll see."

She pulled out her phone and hoped like hell Troy actually looked at the thing and didn't make a liar out of her in front of a guy who was carrying a gun and looked like he wouldn't need a lot of provocation to use it. She dithered for a moment or two before she settled on what to text.

I'm outside.

It wasn't much but she hoped it would have a galvanizing effect. She hit send and crossed everything she owned. In less than twenty seconds Troy was striding out of the room, still in his chaps, unbuttoned shirt flapping.

Her pulse went crazy. He looked hot and he was hers.

"*Joss?*"

The people behind her started calling Troy's name as the security guard looked around. Joss didn't wait for permission; she brushed past him, breaking into a jog. Troy caught her as she threw herself at him a few seconds later.

"Yes," she said, kissing him quick and hard.

He grinned at her. "Yes?"

"Yes to New Mexico and yes to you and yes to love."

He kissed her then. Longer, deeper, oblivious to the whooping and hollering of their onlookers. Oblivious to the fact that all the cowboys from the room in various states of undress had come out to investigate the noise and were also cheering and clapping.

One of them yelled, "Get a room, Jensen," and Joss broke off, breathless and so damn over-the-moon happy she didn't care about their lack of privacy.

"I think that is an excellent idea," she murmured.
"So do I."

Then, much to the delight of the growing crowd, he swept Joss off her feet and into his arms.

Sweet baby cheeses.

"Let's get out of here, doc."

"Yes please." And she clung to his neck as he carried her out of the stadium and into their new life.

The End

The American Extreme Bull Riders Tour

If you enjoyed *Troy*, you'll love the rest of the American Extreme Bull Riders Tour!

Book 1: *Tanner* by Sarah Mayberry

Book 2: *Chase* by Barbara Dunlop

Book 3: *Casey* by Kelly Hunter

Book 4: *Cody* by Megan Crane

Book 5: *Troy* by Amy Andrews

Book 6: *Kane* by Sinclair Jayne

Book 7: *Austin* by Jeannie Watt

Book 8: *Gage* by Katherine Garbera

Available now at your favorite online retailer!

Love Amy Andrews? More books by Amy

Hot Mess

Hot Aussie Knights series

Some Girls Do
Book 1 in the Outback Heat series

Some Girls Don't
Book 2 in the Outback Heat series

Some Guys Need a lot of Lovin'
Book 3 in the Outback Heat series

Some Girls Lie
Book 4 in the Outback Heat series

Available now at your favorite online retailer!

About the Author

Multi-award winning and USA Today bestselling author **Amy Andrews** is an Aussie who has written fifty romances from novellas to category to single-title in both the traditional and digital markets for a variety of publishers. Her first love is steamy contemporary romance that makes her readers tingle, laugh and sigh. At the age of 16, she met a guy she instantly knew she was going to marry. She just smiles when people tell her insta-love books are unrealistic because she did marry that man and, twenty odd years later, they're still living out their happily ever after. Amy works part-time as a PICU nurse and spent six years on the national executive of Romance Writers of Australia where she organized two national conferences and undertook a two year term as president. She loves good books, fab food, great wine and frequent travel – preferably all four together. She lives on acreage on the outskirts of Brisbane with a gorgeous mountain view but secretly wishes it was the hillsides of Tuscany.

Visit her website at AmyAndrews.com.au

Thank you for reading

Troy

If you enjoyed this book, you can find more from all our great authors at TulePublishing.com, or from your favorite online retailer.

Made in the USA
San Bernardino, CA
04 April 2018